The Eye
of the Gods

The Eye of the Gods

RICHARD OWEN

E. P. DUTTON | NEW YORK

This book is for Gordon Sr., Vivian D., and for Kathy

Copyright © 1978 by Richard Owen

All rights reserved. Printed in the U.S.A.

No part of this publication may be reproduced or transmitted in any form or by any means, electronic or mechanical, including photocopy, recording or any information storage and retrieval system now known or to be invented, without permission in writing from the publisher, except by a reviewer who wishes to quote brief passages in connection with a review written for inclusion in a magazine, newspaper or broadcast.

Library of Congress Cataloging in Publication Data

Owen, Richard
   The Eye of the Gods.

   I. Title.
PZ4.09724Ey [PS3565.W56] 813'.5'4   77-24399
ISBN:0-525-10196-9

Published simultaneously in Canada by Clarke, Irwin
& Company
Limited, Toronto and Vancouver

10 9 8 7 6 5 4 3 2 1

First Edition

Separate Events

In the language of the Piaroa Indians the mountain is called Wahari-Kuawai—The Sacred Tree of the Earth's Fruits. In Spanish its name is El Autana. It is sixty miles southeast of Puerto Ayacucho, the state capital of the Amazonas Territory of Venezuela and lies just short of five degrees north of the equator.

When one of my Makiritare Indian guides told me nothing in the world was bigger than the Autana I took it with a pinch of salt. So I was unprepared for my first sight of it. It came without warning. I was in a dugout on the Maraviare, a remote river with little human habitation along it. For hours I had seen nothing except the walls of jungle on both banks. Then by a quirk of nature the river turned and straight ahead, framed by these green walls, was the mountain. In that instant I understood what the Indian had said.

It is difficult for the mind to take in the Autana because it has no parallel on earth. From the bend in the river it was a squared-off rectangular block standing on end, the sort of rock that would catch your eye standing in a field because of its geometric form. But the Autana is no six-foot boulder. It is 2,000 feet high.

The river turned, the mountain vanished and I was no closer to comprehending it when we turned again and it reappeared at a different angle. In the middle of the face, 1,600 feet up, was a speck of light. I blinked and it was still there. The tower was pierced from one side to the other by a cave and the light of the sky shone through its two opposite openings. In Indian legend this is the Eye of the Gods and at that moment I was prepared to believe it.

There was of course another element to the legend which I had dismissed out of hand when I heard it. But now looking at the Autana and the Eye of the Gods I realized that they too had been unbelievable. Now that I could see them as reality that other element seemed real too: the dinosaur. The great prehistoric survivor the Indians called Cuyakiare.

At about the same time that a certain woman in New York City was reading this passage from a book called *Journey to the Lost World,* a man named Jules Smith was entering the Holiday Inn in the capital of the small Middle Eastern kingdom of El Hajjaz. There was no connection between these two events but some events become linked by chance.

Smith had been given an assignment that went against his deepest instincts, considering he had seen enough of jails in his twenty-five years. He had been told to get himself arrested by committing a terrorist act. He went about this inspired by the knowledge that his name would soon be in all the papers. One day he would be as famous as Emiliano, the man who had hired him. Emiliano was the most famous terrorist in the world. Smith wouldn't have done this job for anyone else. Emiliano hadn't told him why he was supposed to get himself arrested, nor how he intended to get him out of jail, but Smith trusted him completely.

Holding an American girl hostage in her hotel room he demanded that the "imperialist puppet" Prince Karim of El Hajjaz be brought to him. He was later informed that Karim was in Beirut where he had been called away unexpectedly and after two hours Smith surrendered as he had been instructed to.

He hadn't been instructed to kill the girl but he did this anyway to maintain his credibility as a man who meant business.

Morgan

1

At the London *Globe* in Fleet Street, foreign editor Don Gordon stood by the row of teleprinters in the Foreign Room with his deputy Rob Kinnear. The news schedules were just coming over from the international wire services to show what stories they would be covering in the afternoon cycle. Dull stuff. If it went like this Gordon would be hard pressed to find a story to head the foreign section in tomorrow's paper.

He lit his fifth cigarette in an hour. "We'd better see if we've got an up-to-date biography on the new Italian prime minister."

"The library is digging it out."

"Good. What about our own boys?"

Kinnear checked the day's schedule from *Globe* correspondents around the world. "They're matching all the wire service stories except for Jenkins in Capetown. He won't be filing on the race riots. He's flying to Mozambique for that Black Africa meeting. Henderson should be coming through shortly."

Henderson was the *Globe*'s correspondent in New York, running the paper's biggest overseas office. All news from Washington and the rest of the States was relayed through it. It had a teleprinter line of its own.

Gordon dragged impatiently on his cigarette. "We've not much to go with."

"What about that bomb in Beirut? It was a huge explosion. A time bomb in an attaché case, apparently."

"We could follow it up I suppose. But it's not the sort of story that'll get Circulation off my back."

Gordon had been a newsman for thirty-four years. He had covered the news in most of the world's capitals and knew the foreign correspondents' job backwards. Now as foreign editor he was in the no-man's-land between the correspondents and Upstairs, as the *Globe*'s management was called. His reporters called him Uncle Don because they were grateful to him for defending their interests against the "business-first" attitude of Upstairs. At the same time they were intolerant of any concessions he made to the management point of view.

The *Globe*'s reputation had been built on solid standards of news coverage but whenever the rival quality newspaper, the *Daily Telegraph,* announced an increase in circulation the *Globe*'s directors brought pressure to bear on the editorial staff to "liven up the news pages." For all his pride in the paper, experience had taught Gordon that when this happened a certain flexibility had to be introduced. Better to "liven up the news pages" for a time than lose the first place. Right now there was a push on at the *Globe*.

He flicked his finger irritably against a yellow memo in his hand. It had a big blue C printed on the top left corner.

"So they're after you again," Kinnear said.

Gordon showed him the memo. It said:

> We are reminding you yet again that every effort should be made to develop exclusive stories of high reader interest.
>
> The need is critical. Since the *Globe* topped 1,400,000 copies two months ago no further advance has been made. The *Daily Telegraph* on the other hand has passed 1,300,000 copies and is still advancing. If it tops the *Globe*'s mark there will be a serious threat to advertising revenue.

Kinnear handed it back. "Pretty strong," he said.

"They must think exclusives grow on trees," Gordon said and turned back to the news schedules.

They were working down the list again when there was a hoot of laughter from Ivan Kean, one of the Foreign Room's subeditors, who had joined them at the teleprinters. He tore an item off the roll on the New York machine and held it out.

"Look at this, Don. Dave Morgan is hitting the big time. He's got a fan club of one."

Gordon and Kinnear read the item.

NEW YORK 12060 EXHENDERSON—AMERICAN PALEONTOLOGIST PAGE FOSTER, 30, LEAVES FOR VENEZUELA TOMORROW TO INVESTIGATE THE EXISTENCE OF A PREHISTORIC DINOSAUR IN UNEXPLORED JUNGLE. MISS FOSTER, ASSISTANT DIRECTOR OF THE FOSTER PALEOZOIC MUSEUM, SAID HER BELIEF THAT THE DINOSAUR HAS SURVIVED EXTINCTION IS BASED ON THE CUYAKIARE LEGEND OF THE MAKIRITARE INDIANS. CUYAKIARE IS THE INDIAN NAME OF A HUGE CREATURE BELIEVED TO LIVE ON THE AUTANA, A REMOTE MOUNTAIN IN SOUTHERN VENEZUELA. MISS FOSTER SAID THAT ALLEGED SIGHTINGS OF THE ANIMAL BY THE INDIANS WERE REPORTED BY BRITISH JOURNALIST DAVID MORGAN IN BOOK THE JOURNEY TO THE LOST WORLD.

Gordon read it again. A woman, a dinosaur, unexplored jungle, Indians. There's a story of "high reader interest" if there ever was one. And David Morgan, one of his own reporters, was the inspiration for it. What's more, he was in Caracas right now, probably the one man in the world this Foster most wanted to see. If that didn't add up to an exclusive, nothing did.

Gordon had read Morgan's book and knew about the dinosaur. Morgan had been apologetic about it when he had given Gordon an autographed copy a year ago. His editor at the publishing house, an American firm, had made him stick the dinosaur in to help sales. There were real enough things in the book, Morgan had said, without having to make a sideshow of it.

The Autana was a legitimate natural wonder. It was a day or two's journey upriver from the Makiritare village. As shown in the photographs Morgan had taken you could see it across miles of unbroken jungle, rising like a great column two thousand feet up, looking not unlike what it was said to be according to legend: the original trunk of the Tree of Life from which had come all the fruits and crops of the ancient Indians. There were caves about four hundred feet from the top, the main one of which pierced the mountain from one side to the other like a gigantic needle's eye. Morgan intended to climb the Autana and explore the caves when he got the time and money.

This whole section dealing with the mountain was one of the solid parts of the book. Originally he had simply meant to write an account of his stay among the Makiritare. They had survived the massacres of the Spanish conquistadors by retreating up into the headwaters of jungle rivers and since then parties of them had emerged from time to time only to trade with the white man. They had preserved their way of life along with a strong sense of their superiority as a people for centuries.

But apparently this wasn't enough for his publisher. So Morgan had gone ahead and made something of Cuyakiare. He had talked with Indians who claimed to have seen the animal. Their belief, at least, seemed genuine. They said the Autana was honeycombed with tunnels and that Cuyakiare could descend through these to the jungle where he lived on wild game or on Indians who were unwary enough to venture into the area. It was all pretty silly of course but Morgan not only pretended to believe it, he went so far as to say that, from the descriptions he had heard, the animal must be a dinosaur.

Privately, however, he admitted to feeling like a fraud. Cuyakiare was just another Indian legend.

Only now it seemed somebody disagreed. Somebody who should know: a paleontologist.

Gordon consulted his dictionary. "Paleontology: a science dealing with the life of past geological periods as known from fossil remains." What a story it would make, he thought.

Trouble was, the story Morgan was covering in Caracas now was big too. That larger-than-life character King Jalal of El Hajjaz was arriving there tomorrow. It looked like he would personally pour two billion dollars into Venezuela. A loan that size is usually made by thirty or forty international banks acting together, not by one man.

And why was an Arab oil producer lending to a South American producer? Just up Morgan's street, that story. He knew the King and the King's nephew, Prince Karim. Clem Cohen, the *Globe*'s stringer in Caracas, was a good man but he didn't have those contacts. Could he take over if Morgan went into the jungle?

Gordon looked around the Foreign Room. It was long and narrow with six teleprinters along the wall where the windows overlooked the famous Fleet Street. There were desks for his four subeditors, who knocked the stories into shape, checked them and wrote the headlines. Each had its own telephone and a litter of copy, pencils, paste, reference books, all the tools of the trade.

At the end of the room was his own office, paneled and simple. He had inherited it from Bill Bishop, who had ruled there for twelve years and was renowned in the Street as a man who never retreated an inch from the *Globe*'s standards.

What would Bishop have thought of the dinosaur story? Gordon smiled despite himself. Old Bill would have run up the wall. Of course the *Globe* was mistress of all she surveyed in those days. He never had Circulation breathing down his neck.

So what are you going to do, Gordon? I'm going to go all out for this story, that's what. Circulation couldn't have invented one more to their liking.

There was only one problem: Morgan.

Gordon turned to Kinnear. "I'm putting Dave Morgan on this story."

"You mean to interview Foster when she gets to Caracas?"

"I mean to go into the jungle with her."

"You're taking him off the loan story?"

"That's right."

"But he knows the King. He was the only one who could get a comment from him last month when that Smith fellow killed the girl in El Hajjaz. He'll miss wiping the floor with the competition."

There was a strangled squawk. They turned to see comedian Kean rolling his eyes and clutching the New York teleprinter for support. He straightened up and pointed a finger, mimicking Morgan's voice with its faint Welsh accent.

"There's no damned dinosaur and you can't ask me to go on a chase for something that doesn't exist. What's more you can't ask me to go into the jungle with a crank woman scientist I don't even know. Furthermore . . ."

Kinnear interrupted, "You know how Dave is always going on about real *Globe* stories. The two-billion loan is a real *Globe* story. A nonexistent dinosaur isn't."

"The dinosaur isn't the story. The story is the search for a dinosaur."

Gordon checked the world time-zone map on the wall above the teleprinters. Caracas was four hours behind London, the same as New York. He looked at his watch. It was ten-thirty. That meant six-thirty in Caracas. Morgan would be ringing room service in the Tamanaco Hotel for China tea to start the day. He called to his secretary.

"Jane, get a call in to Bob Henderson in New York and Dave Morgan in Caracas and link them on my phone, will you?"

Kean and Kinnear exchanged glances. Gordon had dug in his heels. Now for the tussle.

New York came on the line first. Gordon went into his office and picked up the phone. "Morning, Bob. Everything okay?"

"Sure, no problems."

"This Cuyakiare looks like a good story. What about Foster, is she a crank?"

"It was a telephone interview so I haven't seen her, but she seemed a pretty alert sort of person. Sounds quite fun in fact."

"How did you get onto it?"

"She called yesterday."

"Has she talked to any other newspaper?"

"She said she hadn't. She only wanted to find out where Morgan was. Where's Dave been anyway?"

"Northern Ireland on a terrorist story. He's in Caracas now."

"Of course. On that loan story. What a coincidence."

Gordon's secretary cut in, "Caracas on the line. Go ahead, Mr. Morgan."

Morgan's voice came on the phone. It was a striking voice, husky but penetrating. The face that went with it was that of a charming Welsh roughneck in his mid-thirties. It was the kind of face you would expect to encounter in a working-man's pub so people were always surprised to find how polished Morgan could be, especially if it would help him get a story. Gordon was glad he had never had to be interviewed by Morgan.

The voice said, "Hello, Don. Who's on fire? It's barely dawn here."

"Hello, Dave," Gordon said.

"Morning, Dave," Henderson said.

"What's this, the annual general meeting?"

Gordon cleared his throat. "Bob's going to read you a story he put on the wire this morning. Go ahead, Bob."

Henderson read it out. "Somebody bought your book, Dave," he said when he finished.

"Very nice," Morgan said cautiously. "And you both called to congratulate me?"

"Not exactly," Gordon said. "Bob, does Foster have an expedition laid on?"

"No, she's just going down on the spur of the moment."

"Couldn't be better. Dave, how about you hiring a plane and flying this woman into the jungle and taking her up the Autana?"

"You're not serious."

"I'm very serious. This is the kind of story that Upstairs and Circulation have been hounding us for."

"But there's no damned dinosaur and you know it." From Morgan's tone Gordon could see him screwing up his face in disgust.

"That's beside the point. This Foster is going looking for one. They're forever searching for the Loch Ness monster aren't they?"

"What about the loan? It really seems to tie Venezuela in with the Arabs. Suppose there's another oil embargo and Venezuela sides with them? No reporter here is going to get the inside version except me. I know the King and Prince Karim."

"You could get it tomorrow morning at the airport when they arrive. What else is there except the signing?"

"Plenty. Everyone thinks this money is for development of steel, railways, petrochemicals and so on. But I think King Jalal wants something more promising as collateral for his money. Those things won't turn a profit for about ten years, if then."

"Well, what other collateral is there?"

"The Orinoco Petroleum Belt. There's 700 billion barrels there. It's in heavy sludge. It's untouched because they haven't got the technology to get it out. Technology costs money."

"Like two billion dollars."

"That's right. And there's something else too. If El Hajjaz and Venezuela can exploit the Belt together it would change the balance of petroleum power. They'd end up with more oil than Saudi Arabia. They'd be the major power in OPEC."

"If that's the plan would the King tell you about it?"

"He might at least let me infer it," Morgan said.

"At what stage of the conference?"

"No particular stage. Why?"

"Because in that case you can get that too at the airport."

"You're setting me up to get the interview of the century at the airport, aren't you?"

"You know the King. You can do it."

"You mean I have to do it."

"I'm afraid that's it. When Upstairs finds out about Cuyakiare they'll be after me. I'm going to offer it to them before they start claiming it was their idea."

"Look, Don, I don't believe Upstairs understands what these jungle climbs are like. The Autana is hundreds of miles from anywhere. There's no chance of rescue if anything goes wrong. It's a thousand-to-one against this Page Foster being physically or mentally equipped to get up there. It needs a strong climbing team for God's sake."

"Getting up is not mandatory. You know that. Just go and have a bash."

Gordon could hear resignation creeping into the voice and he pretended the matter was settled.

"Let me run over the sequence. You have today, Tuesday, to hire a plane and get the equipment you need. Bob, when does Foster leave?"

"Air America Flight 217. Gets to Caracas at noon. She's booked at the Avila Hotel."

"Good. So Dave, you can meet the King in the morning and then see Foster. That's Wednesday. On Thursday you cover the opening of the talks, then get your plane and buzz off. You'll want to introduce Clem Cohen to the King or Karim before you go."

Henderson cut in. "Wait a minute. Why don't I nail her here in New York and make a contract for an exclusive?"

"No, we don't want to give her the idea she's a newsmaker. She'll be running to the *New York Times* and we'll get into an auction. Just tell her Dave is in Caracas."

Henderson laughed. "You're a real hard case, Don. You should leave Fleet Street for Wall Street. But I better tell you Foster sounds pretty sharp too."

"She may be sharp as hell," Morgan said, "but let's get one thing straight. If she's clearly incapable of getting up the stairs, let alone a mountain, the trip is off. Right?"

"You wouldn't try to put her off would you, Dave?"

"Who, me?"

"Yes, you. You scheming Welshman," Gordon said.

They exchanged a few more words and hung up. Gordon reached for a memo pad and began to write a message to Circulation. Kinnear heard him laugh softly and looked over his shoulder.

The memo read: "In response to your requests I have an Amerindian fable for you, thirty feet high and with teeth to match . . ."

2

When David Gerionedd Morgan first met King Jalal Mutalib al-Kasimy, he was forced to prove himself. He was then twenty-five and the King fifty-two. He had been sent to interview the King for the *Globe* when production of crude oil in El Hajjaz reached one million barrels a day. The figure in itself was not out of the ordinary. Iran was producing four million barrels a day at that time, and Saudi Arabia six. But El Hajjaz had come late to the scene and her production had shot up from nil to one million in one generation. Besides, it was a country of only a half million people, of whom a mere one hundred thousand lived in the towns. The rest were bedouin nomads.

Some Middle East commentators claimed that the people would remain nomadic because Jalal was a bedouin himself. True, he was not spending his vast oil income on Rolls-Royce cars and imported blond dancing girls in the traditional oil sheik way. He had built schools and hospitals. His irrigation schemes had extended the fertile areas of the oases four times and there was a plot of land, credits, instruction and a marketing apparatus for any desert herdsman who wished to change from his herds of camels and goats. There was a thriving fishing industry on the south coast and a shrimp canning factory owned by a fishermen's cooperative. But it was progress with the stamp of the King's own set of values, which were those of the bedouin—bravery, honor, hospitality, and vengeance.

El Hajjaz was a patriarchal state. The King bound himself only by the religious laws of the *shari'a*. He was advised by a council of citizens and by the *ulama,* a group of religious leaders many of whom were of the Wahhabi brotherhood and had resisted innovations such as radio, the airplane and the telephone as threats to their culture. Jalal, on the other hand, saw that modernization could not be stemmed outright. He opted to control it and to take from it what was good for his people. The results had already become statistics. There was no tuberculosis, malaria or trachoma. Malnutrition was a forgotten evil. But murderers were still beheaded by a sword in the town square.

Before he left London, Morgan went to see Sir James Fisher, a former ambassador to El Hajjaz. Fisher told him admiringly how the King would traverse the country with his hard-riding camel train, in the old dress and with the old manners. He would sit with the humblest nomad to hear his troubles, as an Arab king should.

"Duke of Kent came out once," he said, "and the King sat us at a long table in the desert while his cavalry charged right at us. Tremendous show. The King led them himself with his sword in the air. The line of horsemen stopped dead in front of us, reared their horses, whirled and galloped off again. But damn me if Jalal hadn't slipped neatly off his mount and as the line receded there he was alone standing with his hand on his hip and the point of his sword in the sand."

"Very dramatic," Morgan said.

"Dramatic? The Duke damn near shat a blue olly. But the bedouin loved it. You see, they were bewildered by all the changes, the drilling rigs, hundred-ton trucks, oil tankers. Why, a nomad had to hoard his money to buy six inches of steel for a dagger and suddenly there were miles of steel pipelines across the desert. In all this confusion the King was their only solid landmark. That's what monarchy is all about."

The view of the modern young Arab trained abroad was different. Morgan knew the type. They could not understand, as the King did, that the simple bedouin needed a period of transition. They wanted change overnight. They would sweep away every vestige of the old culture. They would try to change the nation's soul by decree. But when Morgan first visited El Hajjaz these malcontents were still only a handful chattering harmlessly in the canteen at the London School of Economics.

He arrived at the scorching port of Alama at noon in a Shell oil tanker and went ashore on a lighter. At that hour there was no sign of life in the port buildings whose frameless windows gaped black and silent through their thick mud walls. The jetty was deserted except for a well-kept 1960 Chrysler and a long, low Land Rover modeled on the jeeps of the British Long Range Desert Group of World War II. Standing nearby were six soldiers in khaki uniforms topped debonairly by a blue-and-red striped *hatta,* the Arab headdress, and a black *igaal,* or headband.

A man in a dark blue robe got out of the driver's seat of the Chrysler and came toward him. He was about five feet ten inches tall and burly. Morgan felt himself being appraised by a pair of dark eyes in a strong face. A classic Arab nose curved down like a beak over a black moustache. There was a tuft of hair under the lower lip and a small graying beard on the point of the chin. The face had a hard dry authority which prohibited informality.

"Mr. Morgan you are welcome. Come."

The Arab stood aside and motioned him forward. A soldier took his bag and typewriter and put them in the Land Rover. A little nonplussed to meet a driver with such presence, Morgan said nothing, walked over to the Chrysler and got in the front seat.

The Arab got into the driver's seat beside him. In the rear seat were two army officers. The driver gestured toward them, "Maj. Abdul Rahman and Capt. Ahmed Wahab of the Palace Guard." The officers inclined their heads.

The car was like an oven. Morgan settled back and sat bolt upright as the sun-scorched leather burned through his shirt. He grimaced at the two officers.

"Damned hot, that. How far do we have to go?"

"Less than half an hour for the first stage. You will change cars there," the major said.

"First stage? Where am I to meet the King then?"

The driver turned the ignition switch and the motor roared into life. No muffler. The major's reply was lost in the din and the car shot across the deserted main street and out onto a baked dirt road along which it accelerated so rapidly that Morgan was pushed back into the seat. But his alarm was momentary and after only half a mile he looked at the Arab with a grin of appreciation. Here were a skilled driver and a well-tuned car.

The road snaked up into low hills and then lost itself in the hard stony ground of their flat summits. The car traced its way through the rocks and the odd stunted thorn bush. The two officers in the rear smiled and nodded to each other when there was a particularly fast change of gears or a smooth evasive skid round a boulder.

Conversation was impossible above the roar of the engine and Morgan held on tight as the car accelerated to ninety up a wide featureless slope that ended abruptly in an escarpment. As the edge rushed toward them Morgan looked in alarm at the driver. He's gone mad, he thought. He's going to kill us all. Only yards from disaster the driver, with a cool born of long practice, pumped the brakes once, changed down into second, pumped the brakes again and put the wheel over on full left lock. The car spun 180 degrees, paused and shot ahead again in the direction from which it had come. My God, Morgan thought, a Bootlegger Turn. Just like the ones the moonshine gangs used to make when they roared along some country road and came face to face with a police barricade.

The car slowed and turned gently toward the edge again. It stopped and the driver got out. Morgan got out too and walked round the hood to congratulate him, all formality evaporated in the excitement of speed.

"For heaven's sake, Stirling Moss, where did you learn to drive like that?"

"From former officers of the Desert Group."

"Bloody marvelous ride. But I thought you'd gone off your rocker and were going straight over the edge."

"You didn't seem unduly alarmed."

"Oh no, just frozen to my seat. Have you any more stunts before I meet the King?"

"I am the King."

Morgan stared into the commanding face and saw it light up with a swashbuckling smile of immense warmth. The dark eyes were surveying him with friendly derision. Before he could recover himself the King took his arm and led him to the edge of the escarpment.

Morgan looked down. It was not rock so much as dried gray mud compacted with stones. It was steep, almost vertical in parts, and it dropped several hundred feet to the desert below. With his rock climber's eye Morgan examined it. Wouldn't like to climb up that, he thought. One crumbling hold breaks and you wouldn't stop until you hit the bottom.

But to the right there was a break in the edge and a foot-wide trail zigzagged giddily down to the sand. It was no more than a thin line scraped across the gray face, carpeted with loose pebbles. To Morgan it looked worse than a line of unstable steps cut across steep rotten ice in the Alps, and there wouldn't be the security of a rope and a belay. I hope to God we're not supposed to walk down that, he thought.

But there was something he hadn't seen, just below the edge of the escarpment at the top of the trail. The King led the way and pointed to a wide ledge five feet below.

"Make your choice, Mr. Morgan," he said.

Morgan looked down and swallowed. Mules. Big bristly mules. He was supposed to ride down where he wouldn't even dare to pick his way on foot?

"King Jalal, I can't even ride a horse let alone one of those things."

"Guests of El Hajjaz do not walk, Mr. Morgan."

There was a finality about the statement that seemed to leave no alternative and Morgan didn't like to be cornered. I'm not going to risk my neck, he thought. That trail could landslide anytime. I'm damned if . . .

"Besides," the King said, "Prince Karim says you're a mountaineer. You were a daredevil undergraduate. Afraid of nothing."

So that's it. It was a challenge. Morgan turned and stared him full in the face. Then made up his mind.

"I'll take that big ugly bastard there, King Jalal," he said pointing to the meanest-looking mule in the pack.

Jalal's dark eyes stared back at him. There seemed to be a new gleam in them. The King lowered himself over the edge to the dusty platform where the mules were tethered. Morgan and the major followed. Above them the soldiers and the captain lined up along the edge. They had an expectant look like a circus audience waiting for the trapeze artists.

The King and the major expertly mounted their mules and sat looking at Morgan, who squared his shoulders and went up to his chosen animal. It was chest high and smelled like a urinal. It huffed a hot blast of fetid air from powerful lungs, lowered its ugly head and regarded him sideways with an upturned eye. Morgan took a closer look. It was the only eye it had.

He had no time to ruminate over this discovery. The mule had no saddle, only a rope halter leading from its leathery mouth around its neck. He took hold of the halter and the heavy beast moved crabwise toward him. To get his feet out of the way Morgan hopped aside without dignity—with no dignity. He glanced around. Everyone was watching with absorbed attention. He grabbed the halter again, put a hand on the bristly back and vaulted onto it. The mule skittered wildly the other way, its hooves scrabbling on the edge of the drop. Morgan closed his eyes.

"Lively animal," he said to the King, his voice coming out louder than he wanted.

The King nodded and eased his mule down the trail. Morgan gingerly touched his heels to the mule's belly and clicked his tongue. It didn't budge. The major with Morgan's bag and typewriter in a pannier rode up behind and slapped it on the rump and it jerked forward. Morgan grabbed the harness and clutched with his knees at the beast's flanks. He leaned back hard as the mule lurched downward at each steep bend. He clenched his teeth whenever it stopped, splayed its two front feet and slithered down near vertical stretches where the trail had crumbled. Behind him he could hear the major murmuring to his own beast and each time the King looked back up at him he nodded and willed his dust-caked mouth into a grin.

At the bottom he breathed a prayer of thanks and wiped the sweat from his eyes. The King offered him a small goatskin of water. He deliberately took only one pull to rinse his mouth and handed it back.

"I always wanted to ride down a vertical precipice on a one-eyed mule," he said.

The King was amused. "I'm glad you enjoyed it, Mr. Morgan."

They dismounted and tethered the mules to stakes in the ground. There were oil drums cut in half lengthways and filled with water for the animals to drink from. An old tarpaulin held down by stones covered a pile of fodder. Twenty yards away was a tarmac road that ran from the northeast to the southwest. Morgan guessed it skirted the escarpment to reach the port from the west. He heard the sound of a motor and picked out a car approaching from the north.

Morgan began to get the picture. The King preferred the route over the escarpment. It was an opportunity for a little derring-do free from the constraints of the palace. This impression was strengthened when the car arrived and a thin young man got out carrying a briefcase. He wore a Nehru tunic darkened with sweat under his arms and across the small of his back. The King looked at him with an imperceptible sigh and turned to the major.

"Time to hand over, Major. Take your patrol down to the port for a swim."

The officer saluted briskly. "At your service, your Majesty." He went up to the young man and gave him the day's log. The military aide, comrade-in-arms and in wild rides around the desert, was handing over to the civilian secretary. The soldier marched off to his mule and the secretary came to greet the King.

"*Asalam-alaikum ya-saheb al-jalalah.*" Peace be with you, Lord of the throne.

"Mr. Morgan this is Asaad Shaaban, possibly the best young brain in El Hajjaz. He's a walking filing cabinet," the King said, eyeing the briefcase with distaste.

Morgan greeted him and stood aside while he rattled off the day's program to the King. He was full of reminders, reservations and corollaries. Every fact was at his fingertips. Morgan noted that he never looked directly at the King, and a picture flickered in his mind of the eternal vizier crouching like a shadow behind the throne, whispering in the monarch's ear.

A second car came up and stopped. A handsome man in his late twenties stepped out dressed in light shirt and slacks. It was King Jalal's nephew and heir, Crown Prince Mabruk Ezzedin al-Karim.

Morgan had met Karim at Cambridge when he was plain Sheik al-Karim. Since then Prince Faisal, the King's only child and Karim's cousin, had been killed when an army transport plane taking him from the capital to Alama had crashed in the desert. The Queen was then fifty and unlikely to bear any more children. After consulting with the *ulama* King Jalal proclaimed Karim his successor.

At Cambridge Morgan and Karim had shared the same law tutor. They had not seen a great deal of each other outside tutorials because Karim ran around with a small coterie of rich undergraduates and Morgan had only his scholarship to live on. But a sort of camaraderie had sprung up between them as it often does between two people of such different types and backgrounds. They enjoyed being together, matching wits. Morgan liked Karim's easy bonhomie and Karim Morgan's drive and brusqueness. It was Karim who had arranged the interview with the King in El Hajjaz after Morgan cabled him asking for his help.

They shook hands now, laughing and slapping each other on the shoulder.

"Why, David, what a sight for sore eyes."

"Mabruk, so here you are in your natural habitat."

"Well, it's a long way from Trinity Great Court and that's a fact. But you're a newspaperman? I thought you'd be a famous barrister by now. The silver-tongued Welshman at the Old Bailey."

"Could you really see me in a wig and gown?"

"I always saw you that way, yes. But I'm not so sure now."

"What d'you mean by that?"

The Prince laughed. "You look a bit lean and mean for a barrister."

"Oh c'mon. Lead me to a shower or a waterhole. Whichever is nearer."

Karim took his arm. "We'll go together. My uncle will go in the other car."

Morgan turned to where the King was talking to Shaaban and inclined his head. "With your permission, King Jalal," he said. The King motioned him toward the car and turned back to his secretary.

Once they got moving, Karim gestured back to the escarpment.

"So he put you through that damn fool mule business. Frighten the life out of anyone, that trail would."

"Does he do that to everyone?" Morgan asked.

"Oh no. He sizes people up on the jetty and then decides whether to come over the escarpment or round it."

"But what makes him decide who's a victim?"

"You probably sauntered over to the car with your tough-cookie pose on and he thought he would test you. Typical old desert-warrior nonsense."

"And how did I make out?"

"You passed."

Morgan did even better that night when he interviewed the King at an oasis fifty miles outside the capital. So well that when he left the next day the King gave him a thirteenth-century brass water jug inlaid with silver and copper.

After the interview the King had asked him, "Do you think El Hajjaz is defensible?"

"Not on your frontiers. But in the worst of cases you could abandon your towns and fall back on that escarpment. It's a natural redoubt."

"Exactly. The British officers who trained my army laid out a defense for an attack from the sea, which was logical then. Later I felt that the attack might come from the north."

Morgan thought of the Narinian Republic above El Hajjaz on the map. It was on the verge of joining the Soviet bloc.

The King went on. "Now I think it might come from within. From the grub that hatches inside. Or is planted there. What is the defense against that, Mr. Morgan?"

He had expected a long spiel on the politics of subversion. What he got was so prompt and hard-nosed that he roared with laughter and quoted it to his closest advisers for weeks afterward. Morgan had said: "Feed the people, King Jalal."

Morgan was the son of a Welsh quarryman. By a series of scholarships he had gone from a village school to a humanistic but disciplined grammar school and from there to Cambridge where he got a degree in law. He spoke French and Spanish fluently and was still scholar enough to enjoy Cicero and Horace in the original Latin. He could have become a lawyer or made his way in a big corporation. Instead he chose the rootless existence of a foreign correspondent because he wanted to see the seamy side of the world firsthand.

Morgan was resourceful and physically competent. From an early age he had loved climbing mountains or sailing a small boat. By his middle thirties he had to face the fact that he was happier there than anywhere else.

There were moments, of course, when life was engrossing. This meeting at Maiquetía Airport in Caracas with King Jalal was one. He hadn't seen the King in ten years but he had kept in touch with him. A year ago, when the King's wife had died, he had sent condolences and recently he had telephoned the King from London to ask him for a comment on a terrorist act that had taken place in El Hajjaz. A man named Jules Smith had held an American girl hostage at the Holiday Inn in the capital for two hours before killing her. He said he did it to draw attention to the oppression of the people of El Hajjaz but even the King's enemies conceded his rule was fair and just. The act had seemed totally gratuitous, which was more or less what the King's comment was. Smith was an American who was wanted in the States on charges of homicide and drug smuggling and the Americans were trying to extradite him.

Morgan drew up in the airport parking lot and noted the soldiers posted at all the doors to the arrival building and the long line of official limousines drawn up with their motorcycle escorts. He wondered how he was going to get the confidential interview Don Gordon had asked him for.

He wasn't even sure he could get near the King. At that moment Jalal was being met at the steps of the aircraft by President Carlos Andrés Pérez. He would review an honor guard and then go to the VIP reception wing to meet members of the government. After a brief press conference in the assembly room he would be swept off to Caracas in a cavalcade of limousines and army trucks. The press conference was no place to get confidential material. It had to be at some other moment.

Morgan showed his press card at the door of the assembly room and went in. The TV cameras were already being set up and reporters were harassing the government press officer. He heard the *New York Times* reporter shouting above the noise, "Will this press conference be in English?" Then a reporter from *El Universal* of Caracas, "*Inglés? Que bolas.* What's wrong with Spaneesh?" There was a roar of laughter.

Morgan slipped around the crowd to the door at the back where Jalal would come in. He opened it and found himself in a corridor leading to another door marked Sala de Recepción. That would be the VIP lounge. The King would emerge from it escorted by his aide and the Venezuelan Minister of Information, Alberto Rojas, and walk down the corridor to the assembly room. In those brief seconds no one else would be with him. Morgan made up his mind. This was the moment. The minister would be outraged and try to brush him off. Morgan had to rely on the King's goodwill.

He closed the door and took the seat nearest to it. The government press men were looking at their watches and beginning to sweat. President Pérez had let it be known that the reception must go like clockwork. An image of efficiency must be presented to the distinguished visitor.

The door opened suddenly and an Information Ministry official rushed in waving his arms at the reporters. "Sit down, please. The King is on his way."

Morgan put his head through the doorway and looked along the corridor. He saw the door of the VIP lounge open to reveal the King, Shaaban and the Information Minister. He slipped into the corridor and hurriedly covered the ten yards separating them. Shaaban rushed forward to stop him and then recognized him. The King glanced sharply at Morgan and then remembered too. His face lit up with the familiar smile.

"Why, it's Mr. Morgan. The intrepid muleteer."

He was pleased to see him and clearly glad of a momentary distraction from the protocol of a state visit. He turned to reassure the agitated minister, "Don't worry, Mr. Morgan is one of my political advisers."

He was laughing now and shook Morgan's hand. "And how is my hard-riding philosopher?"

Morgan seized the moment. "King Jalal, this hard-riding philosopher is hard-pressed and about to ask you an impertinent favor."

"You know you don't have to come to a mass press conference. You can come to see me anytime."

"That's the favor. But I need it now."

Rojas interrupted, "Do you realize the President and half the government are waiting to accompany the King to Caracas?"

"Just two questions, King Jalal, and your trust that I will handle the answers with discretion," Morgan said.

The King hesitated, then nodded at Shaaban and the minister. He seized Morgan's arm and marched him to the window at the far end of the corridor.

"Very well, Mr. Morgan."

Morgan faced the King. He left his notebook in his pocket to show that the interview was off the record.

"King Jalal, is this loan a brotherly gesture to Venezuela?"

The King's eye was very steady on Morgan's face. "It's at $13\frac{1}{8}$ percent," he said.

Morgan thought it over a second. Not much brotherly love there.

"Thank you. Now, second and last question. Is El Hajjaz going into the Orinoco Petroleum Belt?"

The King was surprised. "Astute, Mr. Morgan. Let's not say El Hajjaz is going in. The money is. With the sort of strings you're capable of deducing. But you can't publish that until Monday morning, the day the contract will be signed. You'll still be twenty-four hours ahead of your rivals."

"Thank you, King Jalal."

As they walked back to Shaaban and the minister, Morgan changed the subject, "What about Jules Smith?"

"The Americans are pressing for extradition. They argue that he killed an American citizen in an American-owned hotel and that they should put him on trial in the States."

"What if it's decided El Hajjaz has jurisdiction?"

"It's an open-and-shut case. He'll be tried and beheaded the same day."

Amen, Morgan thought.

They came up to the minister, who opened the door to the assembly room and beckoned to the press officer.

"Take Señor Morgan out through the Sala de Recepción. If these reporters see him with us they'll riot. And take him straight out, mind." He turned to the King. "Please come this way, sir." The press officer knew his job and was determined to propel Morgan directly through the VIP lounge and out the other side. But he hadn't reckoned on Karim. Spotting him with the deputy oil minister and what looked like two officials from the Central Bank, Morgan made straight for him and drew him aside.

"Hello, Mabruk. Suave and sleek as ever I see."

"David Morgan. How are you, old boy. I was wondering if you'd pop up here."

"Couldn't miss the chance to hobnob with the Royal House of Hajjaz, could I?"

"You know my uncle's giving a press conference?"

"Yes, I caught him in the corridor. Shaaban jumped a foot. He must have taken me for an assassin."

"We're all a bit nervous since that girl was killed."

"How about you? You're the one Smith wanted to get his hands on. Who do you think was behind it?"

"Looked to me like the work of a lunatic. The killing was senseless."

"The King said the Americans still want you to hand him over."

"To put him in prison and then let him out on parole? I think it's time one of these swine got his head lopped off in public."

"What a story that'd be."

"Never satisfied, you newshawks. You're onto a big story here, aren't you?"

"Of course it's big. By the way, speaking of work, I've got a question for you."

"I was wondering when you'd get around to it."

"What are you going to do with your share of heavy crude from the Orinoco Belt?"

"Mix it with El Hajjaz light crude of course." Karim stopped. "You bloody menace. You squeezed that out of my uncle."

"Don't worry, I'll send it with a hold sign on for Monday."

"You'd better. You know how delicate it is. Venezuelans are very nationalistic about the Orinoco Belt. The government doesn't want it known yet that our money is going into it."

"Yes, I know. Anyway you can relax. I'm being taken off the story."

"Why? Where are you going? A revolution somewhere?"

"No, it's some damn jungle expedition."

"That's a pity. You know the first meeting of the loan talks is tomorrow morning. We're going to fix the agenda. My uncle won't be there so I'll be heading our delegation. Won't you be covering it?"

"If I can, yes. Why?"

"Well you never know what may come out of it."

The Venezuelan Minister of Finance came over and Morgan knew his time was up. He shook hands with Karim.

"I'll be there."

"Good. By the way, here's a little memento of El Hajjaz."

Karim handed him a ballpoint pen. It was white and gold with the green emblem of the royal house stamped on it. "It's our first little public relations gimmick. It may help you to write an unbiased story."

Morgan perked up at the remark. Just like old times.

"That's the trouble with you oil-rich sheiks. Think you can buy anyone. But you can't buy a *Globe* reporter for a ballpoint pen."

Morgan left the VIP lounge in high spirits. He'd got his interview and a real beat on his rivals. He headed for the public telex booth to send the story and was delighted to find it empty. The riffraff must still be at the press conference.

Morgan composed the story in his head and punched the tape. He dialed the telex number, London 22458, and got the call sign back immediately, GLOBNEWS. He fed the tape into the machine and watched the printer hammer out his copy of the message, first the dateline and time, then the story:

CARACAS 031230 EXMORGAN—HOLD FOR MONDAY. REPEAT HOLD FOR MONDAY. THE INTEREST RATE ON THE CELEBRATED LOAN OF TWO BILLION DOLLARS FROM EL HAJJAZ TO

VENEZUELA IS AT 13 AND ONE-EIGHTH PERCENT, THE GLOBE LEARNED EXCLUSIVELY TODAY . . .

The story ran for five paragraphs and the call sign came back from the *Globe* acknowledging receipt. Morgan tore off his copy, paid the bill and left the booth.

His pleasure lasted until he glanced up at the indicator board as he crossed the arrivals hall on his way out. He saw two red lights against Air America Flight 217.

That was the Foster woman's flight. It had landed half an hour ago. She would be on her way to the Avila in Caracas by now. Time for him to get over there and settle the matter. If he played it right he might still get out of it.

He had already composed his excuse to Don Gordon. Sorry, Don. She took one look at me and realized the whole thing was a fake from the start.

3

Morgan drove across the city to the San Bernardino district where slightly outdated villas clustered on the far slope of the valley. The tall *chagaramo* trees still lined the drive to the Avila Hotel as he remembered them from years ago. The gardens were still trim, the same dark green splashed with the red and yellow *trinitaria* flowers.

The Avila was a relic of quieter, more leisurely days. Certainly more elegant days, Morgan thought, comparing it with the opulence and businesslike bustle of the Tamanaco.

He parked his car, entered the comfortable beige lobby, turned left to the reception desk and asked for Miss Foster's room number.

"Señorita Foster? Si señor, she is in room sixty-two, second floor."

Morgan walked up to the second floor and down the corridor to room sixty-two. He paused before the door, abruptly arrested by the absurdity of his errand.

She actually believes there's a dinosaur on the Autana and now you've got to tell her she's made a mistake and that it's all your fault.

He raised his fist to knock.

The woman who came to the door was attractive. Jet black hair pulled back to reveal a face that was elegant, intelligent, womanly and beautiful. Nice figure, smartly dressed. Moreover she looked like she knew what she was doing. Henderson had said she was the assistant director of a museum. The Foster Paleozoic Museum. Morgan wondered if there was a connection between her name and the museum's.

From her look of delighted surprise he realized she recognized him. She had read his book after all; his picture was in the photo insert and on the back of the dust jacket. Nevertheless he introduced himself.

"Why yes!" she said. "How nice to meet you! I was going to call you. You're at the Tamanaco, aren't you?"

Morgan mumbled a reply. Uncomfortably it occurred to him she must think he had come to wish her well.

She held the door open. "Please come in. I talked with your Mr. Henderson in New York and he told me you were in Caracas covering a story. I wanted to get in touch with you to ask your advice. I really haven't got much of an idea how I'm going to go about this."

Morgan entered and stood in the room. A suitcase lay open on one of the two beds. She had hung the matching top to her skirt in the closet. He noticed a camera and a dozen packs of film on the bureau.

"Won't you sit down? Can I get you something to drink?"

"No, no thanks."

He decided he better keep his visit as official as possible until he saw how things were going. He wavered between the sofa and one of the beds before perching tentatively on the edge of the latter while the woman continued unpacking the suitcase on the other bed.

"I'll be with you in a minute," she said, "as soon as I can get this out of the way."

Morgan reached for his cigarettes. He was wondering how to begin but he could see even this would be difficult. She was laughing and talking about her trip as if it were an accepted reality.

"I realize this must seem very unprofessional but the truth is I couldn't get the Museum to support an expedition. I think you and I are the only two people in the civilized world who believe in Cuyakiare."

"Well, to be perfectly honest, Miss Foster——"

"Please call me Page." She folded a black negligee and placed it in the top drawer of the bureau, removed a pair of blue jeans from the suitcase. "Anyway I decided to come down on the spur of the moment. I want to see if I can find somebody to take me to the Autana and help me climb it. I thought I better do it now before the rainy season begins."

"Smoke?" Morgan said.

"No, thanks." She laughed. She had a sense of humor. "I just turned thirty and figured it was now or never to kick the habit."

"I wish I could do the same," he said, "but I'm afraid I'm stuck with it. Mind?"

"Not at all."

He lit up, inhaled. Exhaled. "Is your name connected in any way with the museum's?"

She had finished unpacking and sat in a chair by the bureau, facing him with her legs crossed. Morgan eyed her shapely calf. Perhaps he could smooth things over by asking her to dinner.

"My great-grandfather founded the museum," she told him. "I guess you could say dinosaurs run in our blood. Which is why I found your book so fascinating. I've always dreamed of the possibility of finding a dinosaur alive and I've never read anything that convinced me of it more."

"Well, to be——"

"Of course I hope you don't think I'm meddling. I know you intended to climb the Autana yourself one day. On the other hand," she laughed, amused by her own proposal, "you're more than welcome to come along with me. I certainly could use your help."

"Well now, wait a minute," Morgan said holding up his hand. He was anxious to stop her before she made a complete fool of herself. "I'm afraid there's been a mistake."

"I realize it must sound a little forward——"

"You see there is no Cuyakiare."

"——of me but——" The woman stopped, looked at him. "What was that?"

"He doesn't exist," Morgan said.

"I don't understand."

"I made it all up."

She stared at him as if she were seeing a ghost. "But your book . . ."

Morgan felt embarrassed for her and tried to make light of it. "Yes, silly wasn't it? My editor told me to put something sensational in or nobody would buy it. As it was not many people bought it anyway."

"But you said you believed it."

"I couldn't very well put in a theory I didn't pretend to believe," he confessed.

Her blush was unnerving in its intensity. "You mean there's nothing to it?" she said.

Morgan shrugged apologetically. "Well there is a sort of legend but I'm afraid that's all it is. The Makiritare haven't got the cinema or the telly to entertain them so they sit around and make up stories."

"But I thought you'd talked to Indians who've seen it."

"They're unsophisticated people. They believe in ghosts and spirits. It's easy to see things if you believe they exist."

"What about the ones who've disappeared?"

"It's the jungle. It's one of the easiest places in the world to disappear in."

She seemed to be groping for something and he offered a cigarette.

"I told you," she said accusingly, "I don't smoke."

Page Foster felt like crawling into a hole. She was thinking of what her older brother Elliot would say. He had been against her trip ever since the morning she had walked into his office and said, "Ely, I've just discovered this terrific book that says there's a dinosaur on top of a mountain in the Venezuelan jungle."

She had explained the book to him as he leafed through it flaring his nostrils. Elliot was an habitual nostril flarer. Finally he had given a snort of amusement.

"What do you think?" she said.

"Not too much," he said.

Elliot was director of the museum, a big pleasant man, handsome in a tweedy sort of way, a brilliant scholar and capable administrator. He was also extremely conservative and would never do anything that might risk criticism.

"I don't know," Page said, "I think the author makes a pretty good case."

Elliot shrugged. "Who is he?" He consulted the biographical sketch on the dust jacket and answered his own question, unimpressed. "A newspaper reporter."

"What's wrong with that?"

"He really hasn't got the right kind of background for evaluating this sort of material."

"Nonsense. He just hasn't got a lot of preconceived notions. I think the museum should organize an expedition to go to Venezuela and climb the Autana."

"What on earth for?"

"To find out if Cuyakiare exists."

"Oh come on." He laughed.

"I mean it. I'm serious."

"But really . . ." He was blushing. Elliot blushed more easily than any man or woman she had ever met. "This fellow is just trying to make a quick buck by cooking up some sensational theory."

He began to lecture her, droning on in his usual stuffy way. One thing Page didn't need was another of her brother's interminable lectures.

"It is well known, my dear, that 65 million years ago at the end of the Cretaceous Period the dinosaur became extinct. Some think it simply got tired and died of a kind of racial senility. Others that it was poisoned by eating alkaloid plants or that a star exploded and it was killed by the radiation blast. But my own opinion, as you're well aware, is that around that time there was a cold——"

"Don't be silly," she interrupted. "You know as well as I do that the cold spell didn't extend over the whole earth. What about Africa? What about South America? The truth is nobody has ever come up with a satisfactory explanation of why the dinosaur supposedly became extinct."

"But what proof does this fellow have?"

"Eyes. Morgan says the Makiritare have the best eyes of any people in the world. He says they can see things at incredible distances."

"And they've seen a dinosaur."

"Why not? I've often heard you speculate that the Loch Ness monster is actually a seagoing plesiosaur that became landlocked after the Ice Age. What's the difference between a mountain and a loch?"

"The difference is I'm not proposing to rent scuba-diving equipment to go in search of the Loch Ness monster."

"Then I'll do it myself."

"Do what?"

"Go to Venezuela and climb the Autana."

"But you've never climbed a mountain before."

"So I'll learn," Page said. "Just because somebody's never done something before doesn't mean it's forbidden. That's what life is all about, Ely. Maybe you should try it one of these days."

She had snatched the book from his hand and walked out of his office determined to do what she said.

But now she didn't feel very determined. Watching her, Morgan was afraid she was about to burst into tears.

"Look, I'm very sorry," he said. "I realize you've gone through a lot of trouble and I suppose I'm at least partly to blame. If it would help make it up to you I'd like to——"

Page stiffened. "Don't bother to apologize. It's my own fault for being so naïve. Unfortunately I was under the impression from reading your book that you were a truthful person."

Morgan was stung. He had been about to ask her to dinner.

The fact was he had always thought of himself, unpompously, as a truthful person. That's what he was paid for. To tell the truth. To remind people that life was a sticky business overrun by scoundrels. But now he was being made to feel as if he had been caught in some monstrous lie. Only it *wasn't* a lie. Because a lie was something you expected other people to *believe.*

"Listen," he said, "I never dreamed anyone would believe my silly little theory. Least of all a paleontologist. The whole thing has been a nuisance to me."

"I'd like to know how it's been a nuisance to you."

"My paper thought your dinosaur would help circulation."

Page faced him resentfully.

"They wanted me to go into the jungle with you to do a story," he told her.

Her eyes flashed. She saw the reason for his visit.

"Well I'm sorry to have been such a nuisance . . ."

He shrugged as if to say, "Let bygones be bygones."

". . . but I'm afraid you're wasting your time."

Morgan looked at her, surprised. He had assumed that all he would have to do would be to tell her he didn't believe in Cuyakiare and she would pack up and go home.

"You mean you're still going through with it?"

"There are Indians who claim to have seen an animal, aren't there? Unless you made that up too."

"I didn't make any of it up . . . except my own interpretation."

"Well, I happen to think your interpretation is correct."

Morgan was worried. Ordinarily he wouldn't have missed a chance to climb the Autana, but not with a novice, and anyway the loan story was too important . . . He had to talk her out of it.

"Look," he said, "I'm no expert but it does seem to me unlikely that a dinosaur could be alive in this day and age."

"I wouldn't be so sure if I were you," Page said dryly.

"But after millions of years?"

"Why not? No one even knew about the Autana except the Indians until seven years ago. Geologically it belongs to the Guiana Shield, one of the oldest rock formations on earth. Conditions of altitude, humidity, soil nutrients and solar radiation haven't changed up top since the earliest life forms. Moreover there's an abundant food supply of wild game in the jungle below. If left alone by civilization there's no reason why a particular species couldn't go on living and breeding right up to the present."

"And you really think there's a Cuyakiare?"

"I not only think there's a Cuyakiare, I think I know what he is. According to the Indians he walks on his hindlegs with his tail stretched out behind and his jaws are so huge that he can swallow a whole dog. He sounds like one of the larger theropods, possibly a tyrannosaur."

Morgan saw it was no use arguing dinosaurs with a paleontologist. He tried a different tack.

"So all right, you're going into the jungle and you're going to try to find him, is that it?"

"You don't have to find him to know he's there. A fresh footprint or some dung or maybe a broken eggshell would do for a start."

"But do you really know what you're getting into? You know what the Spanish say? *El sol pica,* the sun stings, and believe me, out there it stings like hell."

"I've been on fossil-hunting expeditions all over the world from Mongolia to Montana."

"Not in a place like that. It's bloody uncomfortable. You won't be able to bring along any black negligees," he motioned toward the bureau drawer where she had put away her nightgown. "You'll have to eat what you can get too. Ever had caiman stew?"

"What?"

"Boiled alligator."

She wrinkled her nose imperceptibly. Morgan sensed he had found a weak spot. He gestured nonchalantly with his cigarette.

"Not that you'll have any trouble finding alligators. There's plenty of them all the way upriver and they can get rather nasty if you happen to tip over in your dugout. But for my money the most dangerous animals are the ones you can hardly see . . . mosquitoes, *jejénes, zancudos,*" he gave a melodramatic shudder, "crawling all over your body," he leaned forward baring his teeth evilly, unable to resist clowning, "devouring you alive."

He had overplayed his hand. Page snorted in disbelief.

Morgan sat back smiling grimly. So he was stuck. Damn Gordon. And damn Circulation too. He would fly Miss Foster into the jungle and take her upriver to the Autana. If she wanted to climb it he would somehow get her up the mountain. Then he would bring her back to Caracas and do his piece. Seeker Of Dinosaur Disappointed, Not Discouraged.

At least he would see Joaquín, he thought. He hadn't expected to see him until early spring in Gstaad.

Page had recovered her composure somewhat, though she still looked angry. Now that Morgan had given in, he thought, Why not? She certainly is attractive. She might be interesting company . . . if they could kiss and make up.

"Okay, you win. We'll leave tomorrow."

"What do you mean?"

"I'll take you down and bring you back," he said magnanimously.

She stiffened again. "I'm afraid you'll have to get your story some other way."

Too late he realized she was reacting less to his proposal than to his superior tone.

She rose abruptly. "You'll have to excuse me now. I have things to do."

Morgan didn't budge. He sat disgustedly on the edge of the bed, telling himself he would never write a book again. You didn't make any money on them and they only caused you trouble. He never should have listened to Fawcett, his editor at the publishing house. He was a little dictator, always telling you the truth wasn't enough: You had to give them the Big Lie. So Morgan had given them a Big Lie and now he was paying for it.

He glanced up at the woman. She was waiting for him to leave. Morgan took a drag on his cigarette and expelled smoke.

He said, "I'm afraid you need me."

"How do I need *you?*" She pronounced the word as if she were holding at arm's length between her fingertips a piece of boiled alligator.

"Because I'm the only one who can get you into the jungle and up the Autana quickly and efficiently." He spied a glimmer of interest. "In the first place," he said, "I fly a plane and I know where to rent one. I can get us both down there immediately. Do you speak Spanish or Yekuana?"

"No."

"You've got to hire Indians to take you upriver and in order to do that you've got to speak to them. You said you wanted somebody to help you climb the Autana. Have you ever done any climbing?"

"No."

"In other words somebody's going to have to haul you up the mountain and back down again without getting your brains bashed out. Right?"

He rose and stepped to the bureau, stubbing out his cigarette in the ashtray.

"So now, instead of being stubborn about the whole thing, why don't you admit that we both need each other. I need you to do my story and you need me to search for your dinosaur."

Page stood facing him and she knew what he said was true. She no longer believed in David Morgan but she still believed in his book.

The Autana lured her. She saw it rising like a Cyclops glowering out over the jungle from its single eye: the Eye of the Gods. No one had ever been up there and she wanted to be the first.

"I suppose you're right," she said tentatively.

"Does that mean you're going with me?"

"I don't know. We really haven't gotten off on the right footing."

"This is strictly business to me," Morgan told her. "The sooner we get it over with the better."

"Well, if you think I'm any wilder about the arrangement you're wrong."

"That's all right with me. But one thing I insist on. Out there I'm boss. I'm not about to be told how to survive in the jungle by somebody who doesn't know anything about it."

Page had to struggle to keep her temper. "I don't suppose I have any choice."

"Is that a yes or a no?" Morgan said.

"It's a yes," she said.

"Fine."

There was a moment of silence during which each had a chance to get used to their new relationship.

Smashing-looking woman, Morgan thought. Pity she's a bit of a pain in the rear.

When Page finally spoke she had reconciled herself to being a follower. "How do we go about coordinating this?"

Morgan was businesslike. "Be at Carlota Airport tomorrow at noon. Not Maiquetía where you came in. Carlota is in the middle of the city. About twenty minutes from here by taxi."

"What do I do when I get there?"

"Ask the policeman at the gate where the aeroclub is. Go to Bay Five. You'll see a yellow single-engine Mooney parked there, number KTF 2152."

He handed her the pen Mabruk had given him so she could write the directions in her notebook.

"I noticed you brought some clothes for roughing it," he said. "What about boots?"

"I have a good pair with Vibram soles in the closet."

"That should do. I've got a friend, David Nott, lives here. Fellow Welshman, does a bit of climbing. I'll borrow some equipment from him. All you have to bring is the clothes on your back."

"How about my camera?"

"What kind is it?"

"It's a Nikon F2."

"Good, I'll use it for my story. Bring it with you."

"Any other orders?" she said sarcastically, handing his pen back.

"Just be there at noon. We could leave earlier but I'm not going to miss the opening of that meeting I was sent to cover in the first place."

Page felt her temper rising again. It was one thing to accept Morgan as her leader for the expedition but that didn't mean he could get snooty about it.

Morgan walked to the door without turning to see if she was following. He was confident she was.

Suddenly he felt she was not only following but that she was about to plant a dagger between his shoulders. He turned, almost bumping into her she was so close.

The dagger, he saw, was the look in her eyes. Formidable.

"Did you know, Morgan, that your ancestors go all the way back to the first mammals?"

"Can't say that I did."

"Around the end of the Triassic Period there was a great flood and these mammals were stranded in South Wales."

"Actually I'm from the north but it's close enough, I suppose."

"In any event they must have been related to you because their teeth were discovered in Glamorgan."

"Just the teeth?"

"That's all that was left of them after a hundred and ninety million years."

"Really. I hope my teeth last that long."

"I'm sure they will. These mammals were your ancestors after all.

They even bear your name. Because of the place their teeth were found they're known as Morganucodon.

"Fancy that. And what were these creatures? Lions? Tigers?"

"Neither, I'm afraid. They were small furry animals with long evil-looking snouts and tiny pointed teeth."

"Oh," Morgan said backing out the door. "In other words, rats."

4

When Page Foster had run across David Morgan's book in a discount bookstore, it had been a revelation to her. This was partly because of Morgan, who came across as a born skeptic. He had interviewed too many politicians, he said, to take anything at face value. But the evidence itself was intriguing. There were stories that had been handed down for centuries ever since the Makiritare had fled into the jungle to escape the Spanish conquistadors. They told of Cuyakiare who lived on the Autana and of his father, Urorewevaka, who had lived there before him. If this was all there had been Page would have dismissed it. But the eyewitness accounts of living members of the tribe were hard to ignore.

These were always more or less the same. An Indian, the teller, would be hunting near the Autana or traveling through. The ground would begin to tremble and there would be a noise like the roar of a jaguar, only a hundred times louder. Then a crashing of trees coming toward him as if the entire forest were a kind of tidal wave bearing down on the momentarily startled and riveted Indian. As he turned to flee, the great green wave almost upon him, the beast appeared. Large. (Here the teller resorted to exaggeration since there was apparently no living creature he had ever seen that he could compare it to.) Larger than the sky, with a head as big as a mountain and a tail whose powerful undulations cleared a path of snapping and cracking trees behind it. The teller (or so he claimed) never fled without leaving at least one dart from his blowpipe in the animal's flesh, like trying to stop a locomotive with a splinter, and he would stick to this story even though he had returned to the village without the blowpipe, and sometimes without his cooking pot or hunting dogs or even his dugout. There were obvious frauds, of course, eager to prove their bravery by concocting an encounter that never took place, and sometimes there were variations, the Indian traveling on foot or by dugout and suddenly aware of nothing but silence, a terrifying hush from which even the sound of birds and insects was absent, and then the beast would be there, seen in an opening among the trees or on the riverbank, placidly devouring the carcass of a tapir. But always there was the flight, the last desperate dart sent from the blowpipe and the convincing rendition of the genuine tellers that Morgan believed (or said he believed) could not be counterfeited.

Reading his book Page couldn't help thinking of the tyrannosaur skeleton in the main exhibit room of the Foster Paleozoic Museum. The skeleton had been discovered in Montana in 1902 by her grandfather and she had read the plaque at its feet so often that she could recite it by heart.

> Tyrannosaurus Rex. Last and largest of the giant carnosaurs, or meat-eating dinosaurs, and the largest land-living carnivore of all time. This skeleton is 47 feet in length and stands 18½ feet high. The huge skull is more than 4 feet long. The large size of the skull gave the animal widely gaping jaws set with long dagger-like teeth with which it could attack other large dinosaurs. Evidently this was an active aggressive hunter that relied upon its strong jaws and teeth and upon the heavy claws of the hindlegs for bringing down its prey.

Page came from a family that was one of the most renowned in American paleontology. This had always struck her as ironic since her great-grandfather, who had started the whole thing off, had been something of a disreputable character.

Egil Edward Foster had been an Episcopal minister presiding over a rural parish in western New Jersey shortly after the Civil War, a scholarly man with an interest in reptiles, the bigger the better as it turned out. His date with destiny began when one of his parishioners, a neighboring farmer, discovered on his land, while digging marl, which is a sort of muddy limestone, a large, unusual bone. The farmer knew it didn't belong to any animal he had ever seen and in any event he wasn't interested in letting it clutter up his pasture. So it wasn't long, when word got around, before the curious and enterprising Egil drove out one Sunday afternoon in his horse and buggy to expropriate the bone along with a free meal.

It turned out to be the thigh bone of a laelaps, a carnivorous dinosaur, and the discovery created a sensation.

For the next three decades until the turn of the century Egil was in the forefront of searchers for Mesozoic saurians in America. He gave up the cloth and commissioned a wildlife painter-sculptor to build life-sized replicas of his discoveries. Renting an exhibition hall he charged admission to the public, eventually making enough money to set up the Foster Museum. This didn't go down too well with his fellow scientists, who criticized him for being a P. T. Barnum, but Egil didn't care. His attitude was that he was the only legitimate authority on dinosaurs and he sometimes went to questionable lengths to prove it, once even hiring a notorious outlaw to raid the expedition site of a rival fossil-hunter out West. This, and the resulting reprisals, were written up by the newspapers of the day as "The Dinosaur War."

Toward the end of his life he wrote a paper in which, without any proof beyond unsubstantiated sightings over the centuries, he speculated that dinosaurs were still alive in unexplored parts of the world. To his critics it confirmed what they had always suspected: He was slightly demented. The portrait of him that hung in the entranceway of the museum showed him in a setting of the prehistoric world that had finally become more real to him than the real world: a tyrannosaur attacking a triceratops in the background while a pterodactyl wheeled in the sky above. But to Page it was her great-grandfather's willingness to stick his neck out that made him extraordinary.

She had a vacation coming up and if she didn't act soon the rainy season would make the Autana unclimbable. She had asked John to go with her (he had done some climbing in college) but John was up to his ears in work at First National City where he was a vice-president. Page couldn't wait and besides she had had a dream. In the dream her great-grandfather was hip-deep in marl, tugging at an enormous bone. He struggled with it reaching down all the way up to his shoulders, face and beard spattered with mud. Slowly the bone emerged from the ooze and suddenly it popped out: a marvel. Grinning he held the bone toward her, cradled in his arms like a newborn baby.

Now, sitting in her room at the Avila Hotel after Morgan had left, she remembered the dream and realized what turning thirty meant. It meant it was time to face up to who she really was.

She was Egil Edward Foster's great-granddaughter. She was sticking her neck out.

5

You would never have believed two billion dollars were at stake. The Central Bank looked no different than on any other Thursday morning except for the two soldiers at the door with M–16 carbines slung over their shoulders. They were reinforcements for the regular security guard in his blue uniform with a Smith and Wesson revolver in a holster at his side.

The bank's press officer had told Morgan that these would be the only security measures for the first meeting, since the King wouldn't be there. The meeting had been convened to put the final touches on the agenda for the plenary sessions which would start at three that afternoon. It would be attended by Mabruk al-Karim and Asaad Shaaban, representing El Hajjaz, and two senior officials from the Central Bank and the Finance Ministry, representing Venezuela.

Karim and Shaaban would arrive at nine o'clock escorted by two police motorcycle outriders, who would halt traffic at each end of the block while the visitors got out of their car. Two bank officials would be waiting to welcome them and take them inside.

Morgan had arrived with Joe Mann of the *Financial Times* and Jack Brannan of the *Wall Street Journal,* who were staying at the same hotel. They found the news agency reporters already there with Bob Halstram of the *New York Times* and Frank Taylor of the London *Daily Telegraph,* the *Globe*'s main rival.

Taylor came up to Morgan. "Well, well. It's the Wandering Welshman. I'd have thought you'd be in the jungle by now, not covering a dull old money conference."

Morgan looked at him sharply, thinking for a moment he'd got wind of his new assignment. By Taylor's next remarks he knew he hadn't.

"You're a friend of the King aren't you?"

"Well I did a piece on him ten years ago."

"Would you say he's a hard businessman or just devious like a Welshman?"

"What are you fishing for, sleuth?" Morgan countered.

"I was thinking of the interest he's going to charge. A banker friend told me he suspected it might be as low as 8 percent and you know the base rate in the London money market is a fraction over 13."

"Yes. So?"

"Well a loan of this size at 8 percent from one OPEC member to another would really prove that organization is united. The West wouldn't like that, would they."

"No, they wouldn't."

"Look. At the higher rate Venezuela would have to pay $700,000 a day in interest. At the lower rate about $440,000 a day. So King Jalal would take $260,000 a day less to show OPEC unity. Can you believe that? You know him. What's he after?"

"Wait a minute. The interest hasn't been announced yet."

"But we heard you had a sneaky word with him yesterday at the airport."

"Well, you said the Welsh were devious, didn't you?"

Morgan was spared further probing when a taxi drew up and a sharply dressed individual jumped out. It was Euro Fuenmayor of the Caracas daily *El Nacional.* He came up to the group.

"*Dios mío,* look at all theez gringos. 'Ow many from the CIA?"

He began a round of *abrazos,* the ebullient Venezuelan greeting in which you throw your arms around a man and pound him on the back with both palms. "*Hola,* Jack. *Hola,* Joe. *Hola,* David Morgan . . ."

Several more Venezuelan reporters arrived as well as the television men with their microphones and lights, and the scene livened up.

Carlos Chavez of *El Universal* came up to Morgan. *"Mira, Morgan, tu sabes que* . . . did you know the King wants to buy the presidential palace?"

"Ah, si? Why?"

"Because the Tamanaco is full and he needs a room for his camel."

The typical, up-to-the-minute Caracas wisecracks followed in rapid succession, each man vying to outdo the others.

"Oye eso . . . listen to this. The Arabs brought dancing girls as presents for the ministers, who said, 'Thank you very much, but our wives wouldn't approve.' And the Arabs said, 'That's okay, we brought donkeys for them.' "

The reporters punched each other with glee. They paused to watch a white Health Ministry ambulance come down the side street on the right of the bank and park near the corner of Avenida Urdaneta.

"Mira, tu sabes que es eso . . . you know what that is? That's the Prince's mobile harem. Come coffee break he likes a quick bang."

There were roars of laughter again, lost in the noise of the brawling, honking Caracas traffic. Clem Cohen arrived and drew Morgan aside.

"I've just found out there's only three telex machines in the bank's press room and look at this crowd, there'll be a helluva fight for them."

Morgan pulled out his silver pocket watch and flipped up the lid. It was a keepsake and the only affectation he had ever allowed himself. The time was eight-thirty.

"Okay," he told Cohen. "Just in case we need to phone the story I'll go and fix something up in the telephone exchange."

"How about the cable office too? It's just along there across the street from that ambulance."

"Yes, I remember it. We might as well get them both sewn up while we're at it."

Morgan walked west along Urdaneta to the Ministry of Communications on the next corner. He located the overseas telephone section, almost deserted at this early hour, and introduced himself to the girl on the switchboard.

She was a typical *caraqueña* with her white skin and black hair. Her expression and poise were cool, almost prim, but her black eyes glowed boldly at him. It was an enticing combination.

"*Niña, que rica estás* . . . what a vision you are," Morgan said.

Her small nose lifted haughtily at the same time as a saucy grin curved the corner of her mouth. Morgan could have eaten her.

"Señorita, have any noisy and vulgar reporters from London been in here yet?"

"No, señor."

"Well do me a favor and call the police if they come. They're my rivals and they're a bad lot."

He made his plea. Caracas was four hours behind London time. That meant his deadline was in the early afternoon. As soon as the meeting was over he would have to phone a story. But as there was no time fixed for the close of the meeting he couldn't book a call. He would be stuck at the back of the line and his story might be late.

"They'll fire me, señorita, and I won't have any money to take you to the *discoteca* tonight."

Amused, she picked up her pencil. "Okay, give me the number. I'll dial it when I see you come in. You just go to the call box whose number I call out."

Morgan walked back past the bank to its east corner and turned north. The cable office was across the street. He went in, found the manager and explained the difficulty of time zones again.

"If I come in later with an urgent cable could I give it directly to an English-speaking operator? I know it's jumping the queue but . . ."

The manager hesitated. "*Bueno, amigo.* I'll make an exception for a London journalist who has taken the trouble to learn Spanish. I'll show you where to find Rosa Briceño. She is our best operator and *muy bonita* too."

Morgan had his communications set up. He wouldn't have to jostle for the three telex machines. Neither would he have nosy rivals looking over his shoulder as he punched his story.

He thought about his schedule. He and Cohen would take turns at the door of the conference room in case any of the negotiators came out for a break and could be hit with a quick question. At the end of the meeting he would file his story, hand over to Cohen and get a cab to Carlota Airport to pick up his plane and Page Foster.

Damn her. Now that he was into the rhythm of the loan coverage it was doubly exasperating to have to break off for that senseless search. And with an uppity bit of goods like her, too. She had sent him off with a flea in his ear yesterday afternoon. And now he could foresee nothing but trouble. It was one thing to argue with a know-it-all for half an hour in a hotel room but stuck with her for a week in the jungle?

He had had to scurry around until after midnight to get an outboard motor from the Frontier Commission, pack the rations, borrow the equipment from his climbing friend, and drink four whiskeys too many while he was at it, and then get a taxi to take the lot to La Carlota and unload it. And she was probably tucked up with a good book the whole time. Bet it wasn't *Journey to the Lost World.*

Morgan checked his watch. It was eight forty five. Fifteen minutes to go. Time to get back to the bank to await Mabruk's arrival.

He reached the steps and looked around. Across Urdaneta was a three-foot-high railing and behind it a sunken patio with a fountain and trees. It was bounded on the west by the Ministry of the Interior. Beyond that across a side street was the main Post Office with street vendors clustered outside its entrance. There was a brisk trade in *chicha,* a heavy brew of rice and sugar, milk and ice ladled from a churn into paper cups.

A handsome black woman up from the coast was selling sweet sticky blocks of coconut confection and he noted with admiration how the girls walking past her varied from the woman's own ebony black color through coffee, cinnamon and gold, to white. Here and there Amerindian blood stood out in high cheekbones, slant eyes and straight black hair.

He ran his eyes across the facade of the bank. Simple concrete and dark glass. It had opened at eight-thirty and there were already a dozen customers moving up or down the steps leading to the smoked-glass doors.

Morgan had heard about those steps, built since he was last in Caracas. There were fifteen of them, with two paces between each so that they rose at a gentle angle. They were a joke among clients: the first fifteen easy steps to an overdraft. They were wide too, about fifty-five feet across. Some people said they took up too much space in an expensive real estate area.

It was five of nine. Two dark-suited men came down the steps to the pavement. That must be the welcoming committee, Morgan thought. Time to get moving. He was walking toward the group of reporters when he heard the sirens.

Two police Harley-Davidsons roared up the Avenida from the east and spun broadside to the traffic at the intersection. The riders were off them almost before they came to a stop. One ran back toward the traffic they had flagged into the curb to make sure it stayed there and left the fast lane free. The other blocked the flow of cars from the north coming down past the cable office.

The regular traffic cop at the intersection by the post office, following the day's orders, stopped all traffic from the west as soon as he saw the motorcycle escorts. The block was clear of all cars and passers-by in seconds. The first escort lifted his hand and a black Chrysler swept through and stopped opposite the bank steps. The driver came around and opened the rear door. Morgan saw Karim step out and then Shaaban.

The Prince blended well with the scene of big banking and the long black car. Charcoal-gray suit by Widdicombe and Barnes of Savile Row, old-rose silk shirt from Jermyn Street, a dark blue tie with a lighter blue print from Metcalfe and Sons, and an unopened rose pinned to his lapel. His smooth, well-fed, dark complexion was a far more expensive creation, of course.

Shaaban was a failure by comparison. An imitator who didn't make the grade. The clothes were right but he couldn't carry them. You could almost see his scrawny bones moving beneath the quality worsted like those of a hungry dog beneath its hide. His posture was fidgety. His skin sallow. Morgan judged he bit his nails and rolled little balls with the torn-off corners of papers. He was astonished to see the aide unobtrusively flick a cigarette butt into the gutter. Shaaban had been smoking in a closed car with Karim. He really was an addict.

The two bank officials came up to greet them. Morgan glanced at his watch. It was one minute to nine. The Chrysler drove off and

Morgan turned to see the two escorts run to their machines, slam the still-running engines into gear and swerve into a U-turn to speed off east down Urdaneta. It was so smooth an operation that they had vanished before the first cars got into motion to continue their way along the Avenida.

The reporters crowded around Karim and began firing questions at him.

"What are the terms of the loan?"

"Gentlemen," he said in Spanish, "I am afraid I cannot . . ."

"Does your country want part of Venezuela's oil?"

"We want to cooperate with a fellow member of OPEC."

"Are you interested in getting into Venezuelan markets?"

Karim held up his hand firmly.

"Gentlemen, I am happy to be in this beautiful country and I hope these talks will lead to long and fruitful association between our two peoples. That is all I can say at this moment."

Morgan pushed through to him with Cohen in tow. The Prince recognized him with relief and said in an undertone, "My God, they are pushy. They're almost accusing me of tricky dealing."

He nodded smiling at the reporters, the essence of diplomacy. Morgan indicated Cohen.

"Well, Clem here is different. He's our Venezuelan correspondent and I'd like you to—"

There was the wail of another siren. Very close. It had barely sounded before the ambulance came around the corner of the bank in a wide turn and cut into the inside lane at high speed. The vehicle was opposite Karim and the reporters when it screeched to a halt. Its two rear doors flew open and four white-clad figures with surgical masks over their faces dropped out into the street.

Morgan saw they had submachine guns. He thought, What the hell is this, a bank heist? They're going to rob the Central Bank in daylight?

One of the masked men ran to the bottom of the steps and fired a long burst at the guard and the soldiers standing together at the top. One soldier was hit in the chest and fell backward through the glass doors and the guard sat down hard, doubled over with his hands on his groin. The second soldier got his carbine off his shoulder before he was hit. He crumpled forward, his weapon clattering down in front of him. Two customers were hit and fell, writhing a moment and then lying still.

Morgan threw himself on the pavement next to Karim, Shaaban and Cohen. Around them, like any civilians under fire, the reporters were struggling to slide behind each other for cover.

The second gunman ran west halfway along the block and fired a burst at the traffic cop and the halted vehicles. The third gunman ran a few steps east toward the other intersection and sprayed the cars there. In an instant all movement along the Avenida was stopped.

Now the fourth man stepped over Morgan and jabbed his gun into Karim's neck.

"Get up or I'll blow your head off," he said.

"What the devil is this?" Karim said.

The gunman dragged him to his feet and shoved him toward the ambulance, splitting his jacket up the seam as he wrestled and punched him into the back.

It's a kidnap! I have to get to a telephone, Morgan thought. But he shut his eyes and pressed his face into the pavement like everyone else. No good to stare at those bastards, give them an excuse to pump a burst into you.

The two gunmen who had fired at the traffic ran back to the ambulance and jumped into the front seat next to the driver. The other leapt into the back as the vehicle shot forward. It drove fast to the next corner, skidded into a turn and headed north toward the maze of streets in the old La Pastora district.

Morgan jumped up and pulled Shaaban to his feet. "Are you all right?"

Shaaban was limp, as if drained of his habitual tension by the shooting. "I can't believe it," the aide said. "Why the Prince? What will they do to him?"

He was talking to himself. He looked bewildered, confused by the noise around him. There's nothing to be had from him, Morgan thought.

The reporters were getting to their feet and talking excitedly. "Jesus, did you see him shoot the soldiers . . . Look there's a woman hurt . . . *Mira,* how many were there?"

"Come on," Morgan said to Cohen.

They ran up the steps. Everyone was crowding around the casualties. Morgan counted them. Four dead: the two soldiers, the guard, a young man in a flowered shirt. Pools of blood under them all. Nearby a woman, badly wounded.

Five guards came out of the bank at a run and began shoving people away. Police from the Ministry across the street were blowing their whistles and thumping on the roofs of cars to get the drivers moving.

"I'll phone the story," Morgan told Cohen. "Stick around and see what you can get."

"Okay," Cohen said.

In the turmoil Morgan went down the steps and slipped through the crowd to the Communications building, breathing a prayer of thanks that he had already set up the operator. He ran up the steps into the building.

"*Señorita, por el amor de Dios,* get me that call to London."

The girl had heard the uproar. "*Pero, Señor Morgan, que pasa?* What was all that shooting?"

He saw Taylor and Halstram hurry through the door and he coaxed her back to the switchboard. "*Anda, mi amor.* Get that call in. Listen in if you like and you'll hear all about it."

There was a hubbub in the adjoining city telephone section as the local reporters jostled for the phone booths along the walls.

Turning away Morgan went into the deep concentration of a newsman who has to deliver a coherent story by telephone without time to get the sequence down on paper or even to decide on that crucial lead sentence. He stood in his famed position, one imitated in the bar of the Black Swan in Fleet Street by fellow correspondents. He tucked his left hand under his right arm. His right hand was clenched in front of his chin, thumb between his teeth. His head was down, eyes shut.

"Your call, Señor Morgan. Cubicle four."

He stepped into the call box and grabbed the phone.

"Morgan from Caracas. Give me the copy-takers' room, please."

In a moment the familiar Cockney voice of Alf Barnes, the head copy-taker and one of the fastest typists in London came on.

"Wotcher, Mr. Morgan. Go ahead."

Morgan looked at his watch and dictated the dateline and time.

"040930 Caracas exmorgan," he said.

"Okay. I got it. Fire away," Barnes said.

Morgan launched into his story. "Four white-clad gunmen in surgical masks leaped from an ambulance today to seize Prince Mabruk al-Karim of El Hajjaz . . . Scrub that, Alf. Here's a new start . . .

"Prince Mabruk al-Karim of El Hajjaz was kidnapped under a hail of gunfire outside the Central Bank in downtown Caracas today. Paragraph.

"Four white-clad gunmen in surgical masks leaped from an ambulance moments after the arrival of the Prince and shot the guards on the bank steps with submachine guns. In the confusion they seized the Prince and forced him into the ambulance, which escaped into the maze of streets in the Old Town. Paragraph.

"First casualty estimates are four dead and one badly wounded. The identity of the gunmen is as yet unknown."

Morgan paused until he heard Alf's typewriter stop clattering. He went on, "End it there and add this note to the foreign room: Attention Gordon. Will try to interview King for reaction and phone it in with full eyewitness account of kidnap in time for the first edition. That's the lot, Alf."

"Okay, Mr. Morgan. Watch yer bleeding 'ead wiv them bullets."

Morgan hung up and went to thank the operator. He jerked his thumb at Taylor and Halstram, who were waiting for their calls. "Watch these two, *princesa,* they'll try to walk out with a telephone under their coats."

Morgan walked back to join Cohen at the bank. The reporters were firing questions at police officers but one or two had already begun to move away, and the television vans were trying to get through the traffic to pick up their crews. It wouldn't be long before they descended on Los Cedros, the residence where the King was staying, and a battalion of soldiers was certainly on its way to cordon off the surrounding streets. If Morgan wanted to see the King in private he would have to get there fast. Leaving Cohen to question the police he walked two blocks north to get away from the traffic jam and stopped a taxi.

"*Mira, amigo,* take me to the Avenida Principal in Altamira at the corner of Ninth Street and if you really move I'll pay you double."

The taxista drove rapidly up to the Panteón, swerved right and left past the Torre de la Prensa and east along the new boulevard. He knows what he's doing, Morgan thought. Which is more than I do. How the hell to get past the guards at Los Cedros. The taxi was doing eighty along the highway skirting the Avila and as they turned right down the hill into the Altamira district he could see a convoy of army trucks way down the Avenida Principal moving toward them.

The taxi was stopped by a police barricade at the entrance to Los Cedros and Morgan jumped out. He strode up to the police sergeant.

"I'm an adviser to Prince Karim," he said. He flourished the pen Mabruk had given him. "All of us of the delegation have one of these."

He dashed off a note on his pad: "King Jalal, I am outside. I would be glad to help you draw up a statement for the press. I'm sure you'll appreciate it's a delicate matter."

He signed the note and handed it over with authority. "This is for the King. I'll come with you and wait while you get permission for me to go in."

The man started to protest but Morgan slipped inside the barricade and raised his arms. It was such a familiar gesture to the sergeant that he frisked him automatically and then led him to the house. In two minutes Morgan was with the King.

Jalal was standing by the telephone on his desk. "I'm glad to see you," he said. Morgan was about to reply but the King stopped him with a gesture. "We have to act quickly. The Interior Minister has just called me. He said it's all but certain they are terrorists but it's not known what group they belong to."

"They'll probably telephone a message to a radio station or a newspaper," Morgan said. "That's the usual way."

"Meantime I'd better see the press, I suppose."

"You must be careful, King Jalal. You might put yourself or the kidnappers in a position difficult to retreat from."

"But I must say something."

"With all respect I would advise you to say nothing. The whole press corps will be here shortly. I wouldn't talk to them. Let your staff hand them a statement saying you prefer to make no comment until the kidnappers say who they are. Don't even use the word 'kidnappers.' "

The King pushed a pad across the desk. "Here, write it down," he said.

Morgan sat at the desk and composed a note: "King Jalal Mutalib al-Kasimy regrets that he is unable to meet representatives of the press and other news media at this time. He is sure they will appreciate that he can make no statement until those responsible for the events of this morning have declared their identity and their intentions."

The King checked it and rang for a secretary, who entered from an adjoining office. "Make thirty copies of this and send it to the guard captain for distribution to the press when they arrive."

"Your Majesty, they are already here."

"Very well, get a move on."

The secretary left and the King turned. "What now, Mr. Morgan?"

"I was next to Mabruk when they took him. At least they got him into the getaway vehicle without injuring him."

"What swine they are."

"King Jalal, I'm supposed to leave at noon today on another story. Clem Cohen, our stringer, is taking over. But I'll get out of the story and stay here if I can help you."

"The *Globe* is sending you on another assignment?"

"Yes, down in the south of Venezuela."

"How long will it take?"

"Four or five days."

"I think you should go. The Interior Minister told me the entire Venezuelan Army is being alerted as well as the security forces. The minister himself will advise me. Apparently he was a counterinsurgency expert in the troubled 1960s here. I appreciate your offer but you have your job to do. Leave it to your friend Cohen. I'll still be here when you get back."

Morgan hesitated and the King took his arm. "Come, you'd better leave by the side door. I don't want the press to think I have favorites even if it's true." He called to a security officer and told him to escort Morgan out. Then he faced him squarely and shook hands with him.

"I will spare nothing to get Mabruk out of this safely," he said. "You will, of course, keep that to yourself."

Morgan found a taxi three blocks away and drove back to the telephone exchange. There was no sign of his rivals and he guessed they would still be waiting at Los Cedros for the bulletin to be handed out. The pretty operator was still on duty and he was through to the *Globe*'s Foreign Room in minutes.

He heard Don Gordon's voice. "I saw your story, Dave. It's a good one. Where the hell were you? On the steps?"

"On the pavement."

"Jesus. We don't want any dead reporters. Are you all right?"

"Yes, I'm okay."

"We've got an hour before the first edition. Can you phone that eyewitness piece?"

"You'll have it in time."

"Good. Have you seen the King?"

"Yes. He won't make any comment until he knows who the kidnappers are and what they want."

"That's understandable. But what do you think? Does it affect our plans for the dinosaur story?"

The question surprised Morgan. Maybe he could still get out of the jungle trip after all. He answered quickly, "I think it does. The kidnap of a leading OPEC figure in an OPEC country will need all the coverage we can give."

"Suppose it's just gangsters out for a ransom?"

"They weren't gangsters. They were trained terrorists. It'll bring in all the Middle East mess sure as hell."

"I'll cable our blokes out there for reaction."

"But the whole story is here. I think I ought to stay. The Cuyakiare story is phony anyway."

"Listen to this memo," Gordon said. "It's from Circulation: 'We urge priority for the dinosaur story. It will put us up sixty thousand copies daily. We need this urgently because the competition topped one and a half million copies last Friday with a new series on UFOs.

We are printing five hundred thousand posters for Cuyakiare . . .' Well, it goes on."

"But that was before the kidnap."

"I agree, but the Old Man has seen the memo and initialed it."

"What's he say?"

" 'This is in hand. Morgan is covering.' "

There was a pause while Morgan considered. If the Old Man himself had given way to the Circulation boys there really must be pressure from Upstairs.

He shrugged. "I guess that's it then. I'll hand over to Clem and vanish."

"That's the way," Gordon said. "Do that eyewitness piece and then bugger off to the woods with the Foster bird. Good luck."

Morgan glanced at the operator, who was listening in. She was grinning impishly. I'd rather take that one into the woods anytime, he thought as he hung up.

To The Autana

6

What with the grim-faced police at the gate of Carlota Airport and the pushy mechanics around the aeroclub buildings, Page had a rough time before she found the tiny Mooney parked in Bay Five. Ten minutes later when Morgan arrived she saw that things were going to get rougher.

He grunted at her and opened the plane's doors. Then he started checking the equipment that had been delivered last night and was stacked in a corner of the bay. Page resisted the temptation to grunt back.

"Can I help?" she said.

"Bring that stuff over to the plane. I'll load it," he said curtly.

"Yes sir."

She set her camera on the wing and began to bring the packs and bundles to him. Ignoring her, Morgan placed a folded tarpaulin on the floor of the baggage space behind the aircraft's four seats. He went to the forty-horsepower outboard motor lying by the gear, bent down and heaved it upright. Then he squatted to get his shoulder under it, straightened up with his second grunt of the day and brought it to the plane. It took him ten minutes to maneuver it through the loading hatch and into the right position to maintain the trim of the aircraft. He was red in the face and sweating by the time he emerged.

Oh-oh, Page said to herself, here it comes. Morgan turned to her.

"We haven't got all day. These two duffel bags go one on each side of the motor. The rest of the stuff you can pack on top. I'm going to run through my checklist."

Page shrugged as he climbed into the plane and began checking the controls. After a few minutes' work she was sweating too, and her patience was wearing thin. She felt each pack as she heaved it in, wondering what strange pieces of climbing or jungle equipment it contained. She wanted to ask but dared not with the black mood Morgan was in.

Finally she loaded her own pack and called to him through the open forward door. "Okay, nothing's left."

There was no answer.

"What should I do now?" she said.

"You can close that hatch for a start and then go and get in the other door. Put your foot on the step and not on the wing."

Page took her camera and walked around to the right side of the plane. She climbed in and buckled her seat belt.

"It's stuffy as hell in here," Morgan said. "Don't close your door. Hold it open until we're on the runway."

Without another word he pressed the button to start the engine. He eased the plane out of the bay, turned left, and trundled along between two lines of parked planes, turned right and bumped along a track to the end of the runway. He put the hand microphone to his mouth to give his serial letters and get permission to take off.

"Torre de control? Aqui Kilo Tango Fox awaiting takeoff."

"Adelante, Kilo Tango Fox. Go ahead. It's all clear."

Morgan advanced the plane and turned and pointed it down the runway. He held it there and revved up until the Mooney shook with leashed energy. Then he slipped the brakes and the plane surged forward. Before they reached the midway point, he lifted the nose and the plane sailed up into the brilliant blue Caracas sky.

On the left the green Avila mountain range ran from the east to the west horizon, rising in the center to the nine thousand-foot Pico Avila. Below them spread the city, its brand-new freeways streaming with cars, its glass-walled office blocks flashing back the sunlight, and on the hilly outskirts the crowded shanties teeming with black dots of people like a disturbed ants' nest.

They turned south over rolling valleys and were soon flying over empty country, dry bush land with the thin brown lines of dirt roads linking scattered settlements built of zinc sheet and cement blocks, the marks of today's new frontiers.

Morgan picked up the microphone.

"Kilo Tango Fox to Torre Carlota. Course one nine five at eight thousand five hundred feet."

"Okay, Kilo Tango Fox. Maintain course and altitude eight five."

Page winced as Morgan switched from air traffic control to Radio Cacique, a local station, and strident pop music blared through the small cabin. Morgan turned the volume down but she noticed he was giving the program more attention than it deserved and far more than he was giving her.

With nothing better to do she scanned the instrument dials until she found the altimeter reading 8,500 feet and the compass 195 degrees. She noticed another compass on top of the dashboard with a floating calibrated ring instead of a dial. She turned to Morgan to ask why there were two but stopped when she saw his scowl. But hell, she suddenly thought, I've had enough of this. This could be a great new experience for me and I'm cooped up in a cockpit with this grouch. She spoke up.

"Looks like it's going to be thundery."

"What are you talking about?" he grumbled. "There's no cloud in fifty miles."

"You should see the one over your head. Black and nasty."

Morgan rounded on her angrily. "You've got a lot of nerve needling me . . . lolling around your hotel room all morning twiddling your thumbs while I've been . . ." He stopped as if at a loss for words.

"While you've been what?" Page said.

He stuck a finger under her nose. "Well, to begin with, I was shot at."

"You what!"

"You heard me. Machine guns. Bullets cracking round my head. People dropping all over the place."

"But where?"

"At the Central Bank. They kidnapped Prince Karim."

"Who?"

Morgan made a face. "Don't you read the newspapers?"

"Of course I read the newspapers. I still don't know what you're talking about."

"Prince Mabruk al-Karim of El Hajjaz. He's in Venezuela with his uncle, the King. They're here to make a loan to the government. That's the story I was *sent* to cover. Mabruk's an old friend of mine from Cambridge."

"And you saw him kidnapped?"

"Right in front of the bank."

"But who would do that?"

"Terrorists. Nobody knows who they are or what they want. They killed four people."

All of a sudden Morgan leaned toward the radio alertly. "This is it," he said.

Page realized why he had been paying attention to the program. She heard the urgent voice of an announcer: *"Anuncio especial extra extra . . ."* An electric bell pinged six times and the voice rattled on: *"En una llamada telefónica anónima . . ."*

She understood none of it. "The kidnappers have phoned a message in to the radio station," Morgan told her.

He listened, translating the message in bits and pieces. ". . . heroic fighters of the Islamic Marxist Black Flag Brotherhood . . . regret that innocent people have died but cannot allow anything to stand in the way of their struggle . . ."

The bell pinged six times again. The rapid Spanish continued.

"They've given the King an ultimatum. Seventy-two hours to release Jules Smith from jail and fly him to Libya. Otherwise Mabruk will be shot."

Again the bell pinged. Morgan heard the announcer say: "That was an exclusive from Radio Cacique. First with the news, Radio Cacique leads the field . . ."

He switched the radio off. "Damn. Jules Smith."

"Isn't he the one who killed that girl at the Holiday Inn?"

"So you do read the newspapers," he said.

"How could I miss it," Page said. "They were full of it. He's an American isn't he?"

"Yes."

"Will he be released?" she asked.

"The King will insist on it. Some people won't like it. They don't believe in knuckling under to terrorists. The Americans want Smith for themselves. But it's not just Jalal's successor they've grabbed. It's his nephew." Abruptly Morgan seemed to remember he was angry. He shook his finger at her. "The King is up against it and I'm the only reporter who knows him and where the hell am I? I'm heading south on some damn fool search for a nonexistent dinosaur with a so-called paleontologist who believes any fairy tale she reads."

"Listen," Page said sharply, "I thought we went into all of this yesterday. If you want to turn the plane around, go ahead."

"All right, all right . . ." Morgan simmered down. "You've got to remember, Mabruk's a friend. He was snatched right in front of my eyes."

There was a huffy silence.

Morgan flipped the radio switch to the air traffic frequency and held the microphone to his mouth. "Kilo Tango Fox to San Fernando control. Do you read me? Over."

The controller's voice came back crackling with static. "San Fernando to Kilo Tango Fox. Go ahead."

"I'm ninety kilometers out on course one nine five at eight thousand five. How is the weather there? I want to land for fuel."

"*Está bien todavía, pero* . . . okay so far but there's haze trending to cloud. Maintain course and altitude. Out."

Morgan switched off, adjusted the aircraft trim lever, ran his eyes over the instruments and flew on steadily. He looked out the window and saw haze forming below. The brown tones of the earth showed fuzzily through it. They had passed over the Guarico Dam and the only landmark was the road south from Calabozo.

He dug out his pocket watch. Time for the news on the government station, he told himself.

He tuned in to Radio Nacional and the calm measured Spanish of the official news announcer filled the cabin: "*En una conferencia a mediodía* . . . at a press conference at midday Interior Minister

Octavio Lepage said that all security forces have been deployed in the hunt for the kidnappers. Meanwhile King Jalal has made no comment on the terrorist demand for the release of Jules Smith . . ."

Morgan switched the radio off and the strained silence returned. Page decided to break it. "What did they just say?"

Morgan glanced at her quickly. He gave a cursory translation.

"Why would they go through all this trouble to get Jules Smith out of jail?" she asked. "Is he really so important?"

He looked at her again, curiously. "No, as a matter of fact he's no better than a cheap hoodlum, and as you say, that was a hell of a risky job they pulled off, in full view right on the steps of the bank. It must mean something. Mabruk was the one Smith demanded be brought to him when he took that girl hostage. He must have the whole network behind him."

"Network?"

Morgan explained. "It's a sort of international terrorist pool. They've got the Palestinians, the Baader-Meinhof group in Germany, the Japanese Reds. Coincidentally, one of the key figures in it was born right here in Venezuela."

"Who's that?"

"Emiliano. That's the name he goes by, anyhow."

"Oh yes, I've heard of him. There've been a lot of articles written about him."

"And a book or two. He's the superstar of terrorism. The last job he pulled off was an amazing feat. He kidnapped eleven Arab oil ministers from an OPEC conference in Vienna. Hard enough to kidnap one man. But eleven, that's something. He's not a very pleasant sort, nobody you would want to run into. Once some friends of his were holding hostages at the French embassy in The Hague. Emiliano was living in Paris at the time and in order to help them out he went by a famous discotheque and tossed an M26 hand grenade into it. Killed two people and wounded dozens more, including blowing the leg off a young boy."

"How could he do such a thing?"

"I gather there's at least a smattering of political motivation but in his case it's a pretty thin topsoil for what really moves him: money, fame and whatever else can get you to toss a grenade into a group of people you don't even know."

"Do you think he's behind the kidnapping?"

"I wouldn't think so. But there are still several ex-guerrillas here who could pull this sort of job off if someone provided the money."

"A lot of money?"

"A hell of a lot. In an operation like this there are several echelons of operatives, from front men to the hit men who pull the trigger. They need at least one safe house . . . message drops, dead letter boxes, cut-offs. They need codes, vehicles and the cell's own security system."

It sounded very complicated to Page.

Morgan said, "For this one they must have some Middle East operators over here. That means they need airfare and false passports. The team has to be hidden and fed. They need doctors to fall back on and different sets of clothes."

"But who pays for it?"

"There's a lot of money in the Middle East. Maybe that's where it comes from."

"It's terrible," she said. "All those people being killed and hurt."

He shrugged. "They think they're doing right. That's the trouble. It's like an Irish-American giving money to the IRA. It ends up buying a firebomb for some dirty little back-street juvenile, who burns a woman to death in a tenement. Then some dirty little juvenile Protestant takes his turn. Both of them and their supporters think they're right. They don't see the woman burning, of course."

"You hate them, don't you?"

This time he looked at her a long moment. "Yes, I hate them. Terrorists and secret police. Right-wing or left. They're all the same."

He switched on the radio and pushed the speak button. "Kilo Tango Fox to San Fernando control. Do you read me?"

"*Si señor Kilo,* come on in. The runway is all yours."

Morgan landed and taxied up to the gas pump. While the tanks were being filled, he checked his flight plan. From San Fernando they had to follow a new course of 185 degrees to cross 210 miles of uninhabited plain and jungle. There were no lights at the Makiritare village for landing in the dark. They had to get there in daylight. If they had difficulty finding it and arrived late, or if clouds closed in and they couldn't find it at all, they would have enough gas to reach Puerto Ayacucho and try again next day.

Morgan checked his watch. There were four hours of daylight left.

"We're okay for time. All we have to do is find that little airstrip in all this jungle."

"How will you manage it?"

"The landmark is the Guaviariame Island in the Orinoco River. You can see it there on the map. It's just a dot but I remember its shape from the last time I was here three years ago. We have to fly on a course of twenty-three degrees from its north tip for forty-two kilometers."

He paid for the gas, taxied along the runway, asked control for permission to take off, and lifted away to the south.

Immediately they were over the empty parched plains. Page checked the map and tried to keep track of the rivers as they crossed over them. The Torumbo, the Yaguita, the Payare, the Cunaviche and dozens more. It was like a maze. Then she saw over on the left the great twenty-five-mile bend where the Orinoco curved east around the Baraguán Mountains toward the distant Atlantic.

Fifty miles farther south, they were over the jungle and she had her first glimpse of the endless green running to the horizon in every direction. Now the Orinoco was directly below them and Morgan followed it. He had no need of the compass for the moment but to the south and east clouds were forming. Page raised her camera and took a picture through the side window.

"It looks so peaceful. Is it really as bad as you said?"

"It sure as hell isn't peaceful."

"Full of tigers and snakes?"

"Insects. It's alive with insects. They swarm all over you."

Morgan banked the plane over an island. Too big for Guaviariame. Sort of irregular diamond shape. He glanced at the map. It was the Isla del Ratón. There were another twenty-five miles or so to the other one. He straightened up and flew on south. Now he was certain of the clouds. Ahead the ceiling was down to a thousand feet.

"You're trying to tell me that when you set foot in the jungle the insects are at you from the start?" Page said.

"I mean just that. As soon as you get out of the plane a swarm of ticks, called *chivacoas,* will be running up your leg and burrowing under your skin. They live in the grass on the airstrip. If you want my advice, you'll hop out and run for it."

Morgan banked steeply over an island in the river. Its east side was straight and its other side an angle pointing west. It was the landmark. He went into a careful turn and straightened out over its northern point on a heading of twenty-three degrees.

Keeping his eye constantly moving from compass to mileage to the ground below, he put the nose down and descended to four hundred feet beneath the clouds. To Page it looked like he was stunt flying, following the ups and downs of the jungle-clad hills and valleys. Rain began to spatter the windscreen but Morgan kept on course. The Mooney sailed up into the bottom of the clouds and dived down again as the ground rose and fell.

The rain stopped and suddenly there was a river below, an Indian settlement and then the strip. She could see the grin on his face as he gunned the plane up into the clouds in a climbing turn and straight down again, its wings vertical. Page felt herself being pushed into her seat and then the plane leveled out pointing dead center down the strip. He came in ten feet over the tops of the trees and eased down onto the hard earth.

Two-thirds of the way along its length the strip rose in a hump so steep that the other end was invisible. Page's stomach went into her mouth as they bounded over the hump and barreled down the other side through thick, foot-high grass. The shock absorbers in the wheels banged and clattered over the holes and ruts. A wall of trees rushed up.

When he finally brought the plane to a halt just at the edge of the forest Morgan was no longer grinning.

7

The familiar village and the barrel-chested warriors who had gathered on the strip brought two truths home to Morgan as he stepped out of the plane. First, he told himself, the realities of expedition life start right here. Second, they're starting with the two expeditionaries bickering like magpies.

He walked around the plane to the other side. A few paces and he was sweating in the afternoon glare. This didn't improve his temper and he watched sourly as Page stuck one leg out and peered at the ground.

"*Chivacoa* country?" she asked.

"Yes, but don't think I'm going to carry you across it. Women don't rate much here and the Makiritare would think I've gone mad."

The surly retort slipped out before he could check it but Page ignored it.

The Indians were arriving in force now and Morgan recognized the headman among them. He had no hat or shoes and wore a grubby white undershirt and old khaki pants, but his bearing showed his authority. Morgan motioned to Page to jump down and they went to greet him.

"*Capitán Pedro, esa es la Señorita Foster.*"

The chief's hard face relaxed. He nodded at Page and patted Morgan's shoulder. He spoke a few words in the Yekuana language and a Spanish-speaking Indian at his side translated, "You are welcome. Unload your plane and we will hear your news tonight."

"Is Joaquín here?" Morgan asked.

"He's in the village," the chief said.

Morgan thanked him and started back to the plane with Page.

"Have they all got Spanish names?" she asked.

"Yes, but it's only a convenience. It's against custom to mention their Yekuana names outside the family. Their real names are regarded almost as part of themselves, like an arm or a leg."

He pointed to the loading hatch. "I say we dump the gear and go cool off in the river."

He went to the plane, opened the hatch and turned to stare at the brawny Indians. He shook his head doubtfully. "*Ustedes todos se ven muy débiles...* you all look too weak to lift a pack today. D'you know where I could find some strong men?" They crowded around grinning at the impertinence, keen to show off their strength.

"Look at the size of them," Page said. "They're like beer kegs. Can I take pictures?"

"Yes, but hold your camera up first to ask permission. You can't take liberties with them."

Page removed the lens cover and got a go-ahead from the Indians. Morgan watched her deftly adjusting aperture, speed and distance without taking the camera from her face. Click. "Wow, how about that one, he's like a Sumo wrestler," she said. She changed the wide-angle lens for an eighty-five millimeter and took three quick shots.

Morgan lifted a heavy pack from the baggage compartment and passed it to the nearest Indian who flipped it over his shoulder to the man behind him. He grabbed another and the Indians picked up the game, passing the pack along a chain to the edge of the strip. He reached into the plane, gave the outboard motor a tentative tug and slumped his shoulders in mock defeat. There was a roar of derision and a burly warrior pushed past, lifted the motor out and hitched it onto his shoulder in one motion. Morgan rolled his eyes and prodded the man's biceps, and they all laughed. He closed the hatch and spoke to the Indians, who picked up the packs and carried them into the village.

Morgan followed but he stopped on the way to their quarters to show Page the sights. The village's single street of baked earth was lined with daub-and-wattle huts.

"This is Main Street," he said, "in case you're interested."

Again the added barb slipped out before he realized it and again he noticed she ignored it. Lay off, Morgan, he told himself.

They paused to watch a group of girls sitting outside one of the huts painting their faces with the brown, red and blue dyes of the tribe. They were short, chunky creatures with silky copper skin, black button eyes and snub noses, bright pink tongues and a cap of black basin-cropped hair. Below the knee and around the upper arm were wound strings of blue-and-white beads.

"Well, they're not *Vogue* models but they're charming," Page said. "How come they're wearing those little cotton dresses?"

"Missionaries. They were the first whites to reach here twenty-five years ago. They persuaded the ladies to cover themselves."

Two more girls came out of the hut. Their bare breasts curved upward, nipples glistening. "Well, all is not lost," he grinned.

Fifty yards farther on was a round hut sixty feet across, topped by a conical thatched roof that soared seventy feet to an elegant point. The Indians were carrying their baggage inside it.

"This is a *churuata,*" Morgan said. "It's the traditional communal house the Indians used to live in before the missionaries gave them ideas about town planning. This one's for the village elders to eat in and for visitors. We'll be sleeping here."

They stepped from the harsh sunlight into the cool interior. It was lit by a golden beam from a skylight and the soft green glow reflected from the leaves outside the window embrasures and the four doorways. The wall supporting the roof was seven feet high and two feet thick. The floor was hard-packed earth.

"It's windproof, rainproof and heatproof," he said. "And it's built entirely with natural materials. Just wood, leaves and mud."

There was a twenty-foot rough-hewn table with benches where the elders ate. At intervals around the walls, about six feet off the ground, horizontal poles were lashed with lianas to the vertical roof supports.

"Those are the sleeping quarters. You hang your hammock or *chinchorro* from the poles. The Indians don't use beds."

"Why not?"

"The insects would crawl all over you. Big jungle cockroaches, spiders, *garrapatas, chivacoas,* mosquitoes."

He saw she was blinking as tiny black flies settled at the corners of her eyes. She bent to scratch her legs and winced. The *chivacoas* were burrowing under her skin already.

She looked up. "Insects really are a plague around here."

"That's what the Indians call them. *La plaga.*"

"And there's nothing you can do about them?"

"Nothing's any good. You get covered with lumps whatever you do."

"Well, I guess I'll just have to grin and bear it," she said turning away toward a door on the other side of the *churuata.*

Morgan watched her slapping at the midges on her neck. She paused to lean on the doorpost for balance while rubbing her left calf with her right foot. Just how the Indians do it, he thought, an authentic Indian position. Maybe she's not such a ninny. Come to think of it, who said she's a ninny anyway? He followed her outside.

A group of men was sitting in a half circle. Some were carving one-piece stools from blocks of wood. Others were weaving bamboo-strip baskets with geometric patterns depicting the frogs and monkeys of tribal legend, palm trees and heavy rain. Two were cutting gourds to be cured and hardened into bowls and cups.

"All this is man's work among the Makiritare," Morgan said. "The only other work they do is to cut clearings in the jungle for the women to plant."

One man was squatting with his back to them, testing the balance of a blowpipe. He fitted a dart into the mouthpiece, took aim at a sapling thirty feet away and blew. The dart flashed across the space and speared the wood without a sound. Page whistled in awe and Morgan turned.

"Joaquín," he called.

The marksman stood up, a typical Makiritare warrior three feet across the rib cage, the bones of a bull. But there was something untypical too. Page couldn't quite put her finger on it. He was longer in the leg than the others and his basin-cropped hair was less black. Like them he had a hard face with high Amerindian cheekbones and eyes that stared menacingly at the world, but his mouth and jaw seemed more clean-cut and there was a glint of humor in his gaze. For all his beef he was finely-drawn: the odd princely fellow you find among village populations anywhere, she decided.

When he saw Morgan he grinned and spread his fingers, the Indian gesture of surprise. Morgan went to him and they shook hands laughing.

Joaquín's Spanish was rapid and sonorous. "David, what on earth . . . What are you doing here?"

"Just thought I'd drop in and say hello."

"I saw the plane come in but I thought it was the usual bunch of anthropologists."

"You're not far off."

They stood laughing and smiling at each other.

"I didn't expect to see you until March," Joaquín said. "Are we all set for skiing?"

"We're booked at the Inn. I hear the snow's excellent."

"You should have let me know you were coming. I would have arranged a hunt."

"I didn't know I was going to be here. I was in Caracas on a story and something came up."

"So I see," Joaquín eyed Page at a distance.

Morgan glanced at her over his shoulder. "Unfortunately we're barely speaking. She's a paleontologist. Believes in Cuyakiare. Thinks he's a dinosaur."

"She's read your book."

"Mm," Morgan grunted. "She wants to climb the Autana."

"Has she ever climbed before?"

"No, that's just it. She's never climbed and she thinks it's going to be a lark getting up a monster like that. The *Globe* thinks it'll make a good story. Search for dinosaur and all that. Anyway, now that I'm here I might as well try it. Want to join us?"

"I think I'll leave the climbing to you. I wouldn't want to interfere with you and your lady friend."

Morgan grunted again. "You'll come upriver with us, won't you?"

"Sure, I've been wanting to do some hunting up around there, but most of the men here are afraid to come with me. There's a couple of boys, though, who might go if you make it worth their while. Want me to ask them?"

"Would you do that? In the meantime I assume you'll want to play the noble savage for my friend until you're better acquainted."

Page saw them laughing together and looking toward her, not unkindly but privately all the same. She went over and Morgan introduced them.

"This is Joaquín, one of the tribe's most renowned warriors. *Y esa es la Señorita Foster.*"

Joaquín shook her hand. "*Mucho gusto.*" Morgan and he exchanged a few more words in Spanish and then he strode off toward the river.

"He's coming with us to the foot of the Autana. He's gone to arrange for a boat."

"You and he must be good friends."

"We've known each other a long time. He's an unusual character."

"How do you mean?"

Morgan picked up the blowpipe to change the subject. "If you really want to see something ingenious look at this." The blowpipe was long but light. "It's not a single tube. There's one tube inside another."

"Yes, I see."

"The inside tube is called a *curata*. It's a sort of giant bamboo grass which grows at the base of the Marawaka plateau and nowhere else, maybe a week's journey from here. According to legend it's the wing bones of the giant *dimoshi,* a sacred bird that crashed into the mountain and fell into the jungle. It's the only plant that grows long enough for a blowpipe without joints along it that would block the dart."

"What about the outer tube?"

"That was easier to find. It's from the *yurua* palm, cut when it's about fifteen feet high. They leave it for a month while termites eat away the pulp inside. Then a *curata* of the right width is pushed into it and there's your blowpipe."

"But why not just the *curata* or the *yurua* alone?" she asked.

"That's where Makiritare genius comes in. The palm provides the rigidity the bamboo doesn't have. The bamboo gives the smooth bore the palm doesn't have."

Morgan was enjoying showing off his knowledge. "That's not all," he said. "The two tubes are soldered together with a black resin from the *mani* tree. The mouthpiece is made from the seed case of the *ashadu* palm and stuck on with the same stuff. You couldn't break it off if you tried."

Page took the weapon and examined it, touching and even sniffing it. She won't miss much at that rate, he thought, she'll be tasting the bloody thing next.

He went to the sapling and pulled out the dart. He needed two hands because it had gone in one and a half inches. It was a foot long and a tenth of an inch in diameter. Like a deadly splinter. He brought it to her.

"This is called a *cunwa*. It's made from the fibers of the *wasai* palm, which have to be dried and straightened."

Page pointed to a cone-shaped tuft of white fibers on the shaft two inches from the blunt end. "What's this?"

"That's like the feathers on an arrow. It's made of hairs from kapok seed and rolled to the same diameter as the tube so it has a piston effect when it's blown through it."

Page took the dart and Morgan watched her again as she scrutinized it. "Look," she said, "there's a tiny ring scored around it near the point."

"That bit breaks off in the wound. When you're hunting for your dinner you want to be sure you get it."

"Why is the point colored black?"

"That's dried curare poison. It's used only for big game like deer. The Makiritare don't make curare. They get it from the Piaroa tribe."

He saw Page shiver and he spoke up for his Indians. "Curare has a sinister sound for us because of stories about murderous sneaky savages. But if you had to feed your family and somebody offered you a chemical compound that paralyzes the diaphragm of a big animal so that it asphyxiates, you wouldn't feel any worse about it than you do about a knife and fork."

"I suppose not," she said.

Morgan was beginning to think he had missed his calling. He should have been a tour guide. "How about that swim?" he said.

They went into the *churuata* to get soap and towels. "Did I tell you about the famous black waters of this region? They're gold and ruby in the shallows and jet black where it's deep. Something to do with minerals. And it's so pure you can drink it as you swim."

"Lead me to it. Maybe it'll drown the *chivacoas.*"

"No such luck, but it'll ease the itch a bit."

Page threw a towel around her neck. "What do we wear by the way?"

"It's best to follow the customs here. As you've seen, bare buttocks are two a penny so a man can show off his rear end if he thinks it's worth it, but he has to cover up in front. It's an offense to show his Johnny Wobbler."

"Johnny Wobbler?"

"You haven't got one so you don't have to worry."

"So what does a woman wear?"

"You could go in your shirt and pants, I suppose, but if you really want to do it the Indian way you'll go like the other women."

"How's that?"

"Naked stern and bare bosom," he said nonchalantly.

Without waiting for a reply he led the way across the village and down the riverbank to where a flat rock jutted into the water.

Downstream the river broke into half a mile of rapids. Upstream it curved in a wide bend three hundred yards across with a crystal-clear reflection of the trees on the banks. There was no sound except the soft melodic note of a bird.

Morgan stripped to his shorts and plunged in. He smiled to himself underwater. He knew she wouldn't take him up on his dare, he hadn't expect her to. But the thought was amusing. He surfaced and looked back.

On the bank Page was performing an elaborate striptease routine. She undulated out of her blue jeans as if they were red satin and black lace. She slipped off her bush jacket and tossed it aside with a bump, undid her bra with a grind. Raising her arms she wound her black hair into a topknot. In her cotton panties she was stunning: lissome, gleaming, rounded, feline and womanly. What's more, her act was funny.

Morgan silently acknowledged he was beaten. She dove into the river and he swam to her. They both crawled out onto the flat rock. For a while he said nothing. Then he faced her.

"You win, Page."

"Page?" she said. They were finally on a first-name basis?

"Yes," Morgan said. "You can certainly rise to the occasion."

"Thanks."

"I'm sorry I've been such a grouch. How about a truce?"

"You mean we're friends?"

"I hope so."

"Well, it's about time. Shake hands . . . David."

They shook hands and laughed. Morgan looked around at the approaching dusk.

"It's about mosquito time too," he said. "I hate to say it but you should cover up those marvelous tits."

It wasn't until after dinner in the *churuata* that night that Page had a chance to ask about Cuyakiare.

The elders had gathered around the table soon after dark. She was sitting opposite the chief and Morgan and Joaquín were on her right. On her left a withered old man stared at her intently.

"Somebody's giving me the eye," she said.

"In all his life he's never seen a woman eating with the men," Morgan told her. "You better behave."

The women brought the food in from their cooking fires outside. They laid it on the table quietly and went out again to watch from the doorway. When one of the men wanted more he held his bowl out behind him and a woman came in to fill it. He neither looked at her nor spoke.

They ate chicken stewed with corn and manioc, and fish fried in palm oil. Joaquín showed Page how to break up the cassava biscuit with her fingers and soften it in the gourd of water in front of her. He passed her an old rum bottle filled with a thick dark mixture, *"Prueba eso . . ."*

Morgan translated. "It's a hot sauce, a real Makiritare delicacy. Try it."

Page tipped a few drops onto her fish and tasted it. It was piquant with a flavor she couldn't place. "What's it made of?"

"*Míralo contra la luz,*" Joaquín said.

"He says you should look at it against the light."

She held the bottle up to the candle and gasped. It was full of dead ants.

"They're *bachaco* ants and it's their sting that gives the tang."

Through his interpreter sitting behind him the chief asked the reason for their visit. Morgan said they wanted to get closer to the Autana than he had three years ago. He didn't say they intended to climb it; the old man would have found this difficult to understand. As it was he shook his head and frowned, muttering to the interpreter.

Page heard the word "Cuyakiare." This was her chance. She threw her arms wide in a gesture of inquiry.

"Cuyakiare?" she said.

There was a stir among the Indians. The chief considered her and raised his hand for silence. Through the interpreter he spoke and Morgan translated.

"In the days when there were only gods, El Autana rose to the sky and spread into the Great Tree of Life. From this tree came all the fruits on earth. Men came and ate fruit they did not need and threw it on the ground. The angry gods struck down the tree. The Autana is the stump of its trunk.

"The hole that pierces the mountain is the Eye of the Gods with which they watch the deeds of the men who misused the fruits that had been given them.

"Cuyakiare lives in the Eye of the Gods. Those who trespass near it sometimes never return.

"He is as high as six men and he walks like thunder. He is as old as the world."

There was a murmur of approval from the elders.

"He can certainly put over a tall story," Morgan said.

"You've been brainwashed is all," Page said. "You were told in school that dinosaurs are extinct and you can't see it any other way. The coelacanth was supposed to be extinct too, you know."

"So?"

"So they found one swimming around off Africa in 1952."

"Well maybe the coelacanth, whatever it is, was more adaptable."

"You'd have to go a long way to find something more adaptable than the dinosaur. Do you know how long he ruled the earth?"

"I give up."

"A hundred and forty million years. That's quite a bit more than the four million years that man has been around."

Morgan was impressed.

"What's more," Page said, "there were hundreds of different species, an incredible variety, plant eaters and meat eaters, all sizes and shapes, some as tall as a three-story building, others small enough to pick up in your hand."

"Then why did he disappear?"

"No one knows for sure. It wasn't until the nineteenth century that people even began to be aware that there had ever even been such a thing as a dinosaur."

"They found the bones," Morgan said.

"That's right. They didn't know what to make of them at first. Then, finally, in the 1840s someone proposed that a new order of reptiles be established—Dinosauria, which means 'terrible lizard.' "

"I still can't buy it. How could a dinosaur be on the Autana? How could it have reproduced itself all these millions of years?"

"Morgan, you surprise me. Didn't your daddy ever tell you about the birds and the bees?"

"Yes, and he told me you need two of them to make another one."

"So, if the Autana is as honeycombed with tunnels as the Indians believe, there could be a whole lost world inside it. And speaking of birds, the best proof that the dinosaur has survived up to the present, at least in one form, is in your stomach right now."

"How's that?"

"There was one dinosaur called archaeopteryx that was halfway between a reptile and a bird. In other words that chicken you had for dinner tonight was the direct descendant of a dinosaur."

"I thought there was something prehistoric about it," he said.

The Indians had begun to leave for their huts and the chief came around the table and pointed to the skylight above them. "Cuyakiare high like that," he said in halting Spanish.

Morgan translated and burst into a laugh at the triumph on Page's face.

"What a princely con man he is."

He walked to the door with Joaquín and came back to Page. "He'll have the dugout ready before dawn. Come on, we'll sort out the kit."

They went to their baggage and Morgan put two empty duffel bags on the floor. "We'll wear all our climbing equipment when we start up the mountain. The rest of the gear goes in these packs. Personal stuff in one, food in the other. You're allowed one spare shirt, your parka and sleeping bag. So forget your clean socks and nice woolly sweater. Got it?"

"Yes. This is Genghis Khan's light infantry."

"It's worse than that. I have to haul those packs up the mountain as well as you."

He laid out their equipment next to the duffel bags and Page ran her eyes over it. Two shirts, two sleeping bags, two parkas, two flashlights, two . . .

"What are those things?" she said pointing to two bundles of black nylon material.

"Oh, that's a contraption called a bat tent invented by the notorious Batso Harding."

"Batso?"

"That's what he's called. Real name's Warren."

"Warren Harding was a president."

"Batso Harding is a president. President of the Lower Sierra Eating, Drinking and Farcing Society. He's also a demon climber and this thing is one of his most devilish devices."

She peered at him suspiciously. "If I'm going to use one I want to know about it."

"You've got to know about it. You might have to sleep in it."

He picked up a bat tent and shook it out. It was a six-foot-long rectangle of nylon which dangled from ten webbing tapes like an upside-down parachute. The ends of the tapes were joined in a loop into which Morgan clipped a steel alloy snaplink, or carabiner as climbers call them. He clipped this onto a wooden peg in a roof beam. The rectangle hung down about two feet from the floor.

"It looks like a great bat hanging there," Page said.

"Exactly. This part of it is the hammock. When we put a nylon sheet over it it becomes a bat tent."

"What do you hang it from on a climb?"

"You hammer one of these steel spikes called pitons into a crack and clip the carabiner in."

"But what's below you?"

"Space."

"How much space?"

"Depends how far up the wall you are. Five hundred feet, a thousand feet, two thousand feet."

"Morgan . . ."

"Yes?"

"You're putting me on."

"No, I'm not. Until Batso came along climbers used to sleep hanging in their harness if no ledge was handy. Come and try it."

She struggled into the hammock and stretched out face upward.

"That's it," Morgan said. "These support tapes come down from the piton in two pairs and one single loop. The single loop goes under your heels and holds your feet up. Of the pair of tapes at the other end one goes under your head and the other under your neck." He sorted the tapes. "Now the middle pair. One goes under the bottom of your spine and the other where your rear end meets the top of your legs. Right here."

A muffled voice from inside the hammock said what sounded to him like "Take your hand off my fanny." He ignored it.

"How's it feel? Wriggle about so you're confident it will hold you."

Page wriggled. "It's very clever. I'm almost horizontal."

"Batso is quite fond of being horizontal. In one way or another."

Morgan didn't tell her that few climbers ever attempt a rock wall so sheer that they have to use a bat tent. The bat tent was designed for one point of support because on some climbs that was all that was available. If the single piton pulled out you had had it.

Page's face was hidden by the sides of the hammock but he could see her shape outlined in black nylon underneath. An idea sprang from a corner of his mind. How about making love in one of these a thousand feet off the ground?

Now *that* is a perilous, spellbinding notion, he thought.

8

They had left the *churuata* in the dark and loaded by flashlight. Now as they shoved off from the bank and turned upriver it was beginning to get light. Joaquín started the outboard motor and the *curiara* lifted its bow and planed across the satiny black surface. They were underway.

In the bow a young tribesman was looking out for rocks or floating logs. Behind him, singing in the toneless Makiritare way, sat his brother, the second crewman. In the middle was the pile of baggage, rations and climbing gear. Then Morgan and Page facing each other. Behind Page was a drum of gasoline and then Joaquín, the pilot.

It was a clear fresh morning. Even the motor wasn't offensive, Morgan thought, and it would shorten their journey from four days to twelve hours.

But something was bothering him about those twelve short hours. . . . He balanced a butane stove on the bottom of the *curiara* and lit it. Scooping up a quart of river water in a can he was soon percolating aromatic Venezuelan coffee through a scrap of cloth. He handed a mugful to Page, along with a chunk of cassava.

"Breakfast."

"Mm, thanks. I can't wait to see the Autana."

She was smiling excitedly and Morgan realized what was troubling him. He settled back against the baggage and thought, So you've done it again.

He looked at Page, admiring the slash of raven hair skirting her smooth white cheekbone. She was sipping her coffee and watching the jungle go by. What was he going to do? She expected to climb the Autana and now with only twelve hours separating them from the mountain he was beginning to face up to how difficult it was going to be.

He recalled the language of his old army climbing manual. How did it go?

"All the surfaces of a rock face—walls, cracks, chimneys, slabs—need a different technique. More important, you must be mentally prepared."

So in the next twelve hours he was going to have to teach Page all the essential techniques for getting up a rock face and "mentally" prepare her as well. It was no comfort to know that they would be tackling something that had never been climbed before, something as intimidating as the Autana.

Well, perhaps she would be so clumsy in practice that he would call the whole thing off . . . make it easy on him.

"What are you wrinkling your forehead about?" she said.

"Huh? . . . Oh, nothing."

They went on, here and there passing a *caney* on the bank, father fishing and mother beating clothes at the water's edge with her children beside her. White herons flapped slowly downriver, a pair of guacamayas in their red-and-green plumage rose from a tree with a startled screech. As they rounded the bends close to the bank Morgan gazed down through the clear red water at the bright green-and-yellow reeds on the bottom.

Once before he had undertaken a difficult climb with someone who had never climbed before. It was the ascent of the face of Angel Falls, the highest waterfall in the world, three thousand feet of vertical walls. But his partner had been in superior condition and was a natural-born athlete and daredevil. Morgan remembered the baking rock and dust-dry lichen on the Angel turning to slime in the sudden rain. Like oil on the track for a racing-car driver. He thought of another phrase from the manual. "In most games if you lose, you lose a point or a run. In climbing you may lose your——"

"*Yadiwe, yadiwe!*" the lookout shouted suddenly. "Alligator!"

Joaquín rammed the *curiara* onto a flat rock, grabbed his machete, and dashed ashore. The two brothers had leaped out and were racing across the shallows yelling, "*Aka'de tu'mane . . .* quick, over here!"

Morgan pulled Page out and followed them. "Hurry, we can't miss this."

He stopped at the edge of a shallow pool in the rocks where the alligator had been sunning itself when the lookout first sighted it. The brothers had cornered it. The alligator made a dash to slip over the edge into deep water and they headed it off, dancing in front of it, yelling and splashing to confuse it, hopping aside as it snapped at their legs. One slipped and as the alligator went for him the other thumped it in the side with his heel. It whirled and the fallen boy jumped to his feet. Morgan saw it was only a matter of seconds before somebody would lose a limb.

But Joaquín was already dashing in. He had cut a ten-foot pole from a sapling and sharpened a point. Plunging the point into the alligator's back he threw all his weight on it while one of the brothers grabbed the machete and chopped hard where the base of the skull met the horny hide of the neck. As he kept chopping, the pinned alligator's struggles grew weaker. There was a final twitch of its heavy tail and then the brothers were jumping about, slapping each other on the shoulder and laughing.

In the hubbub Morgan became aware of a clicking sound and he turned to Page in surprise.

"I didn't realize you had your camera. Did you get any pictures?"

"Yup," she said.

"What about when the boy fell in front of it?"

"Of course."

"If it had charged you, would you have taken a picture of that too?"

"Damn right. Snap first, run later is my motto."

Morgan saw it wouldn't be so easy keeping her off the Autana after all.

"I believe you would," he said.

Morgan helped the brothers heave the alligator onto Joaquín's back. Between them they wrestled it back to the *curiara,* where Joaquín prepared to gut and quarter it.

"That was some fight," Morgan said to him in Spanish.

"If he had been any bigger we'd never have got him. He was all we could handle."

Morgan watched him thrust his knife into the belly under the rib cage and cut down to the legs through the tough scales. The guts were dumped into the river and vanished.

Joaquín looked up. "How'd you like to help me cut him up for the pot?"

"No thanks. You're doing fine. You should have been a butcher."

"They didn't give a degree in it where I went to school."

"That's right, I keep forgetting you went to one of those fancy Ivy League establishments."

Joaquín raised a bloody hand and sang, *"Somos tres corderitos que hemos perdido el camino . . .* bah, bah, bah."

"What's that he's singing?" Page asked.

"Oh, it's just an old native tune," Morgan said.

As they continued upriver the brothers were still talking about their adventure. *"Hombre casi te comío la pata . . .* it almost bit your leg off. I'm sick with laughing."

Morgan passed a big pot to them. *"Mira locos . . .* fill that with water before you pass out."

He took the pot from them and placed it on the stove. In went gobs of white flesh with the shiny green belly scales attached. He washed the rest off, head, tail, legs and body, at the side of the *curiara* and stacked the pieces in the bottom. Glancing up he saw Page watching him with a sickly look. It occurred to him she was more afraid of a dead alligator than a live one.

"What are you doing?" she asked.

"Making lunch."

"I thought so."

"Why, you hungry? We won't be eating for a couple of hours."

"I can't wait," she said grimly.

One hour later they came to a slab of pink rock, big as a tennis court, shelving gently into the water on the right bank.

Morgan sat up. "That's José's landing place. His hut is in the trees."

Joaquín cut the motor and the *curiara* glided in and ran up onto the rock. They stepped out and followed the Indians across to a trail on the left.

"José's a good man," Morgan told Page. "Last time I was with him the outboard motor went dead and we settled back for a slow drift downstream. But we ran into an electric storm that lasted twenty-six hours. The rain was so heavy we couldn't see a thing. Never seen such lightning, one flash after another, and the thunder sounded like big naval guns."

There was a clearing ahead of them and Morgan heard dogs barking and children babbling excitedly.

"Anyway José sat in the prow for twenty-six hours with his steering paddle while the rest of us cowered under a tarpaulin. Then we drifted four more days without food because I hadn't reckoned on that sort of accident. José never said a word."

They came to a big palm hut and he led Page inside.

"He has a great sense of order for an Indian. Look at the way his house is laid out."

At one end was a long table and a bench with cooking pots lined up on it. Next came a living area with polished log blocks as seats. Then the sleeping quarters with several hammocks hanging from poles. The hard-earth floor was swept clean.

Three naked children appeared shyly and Morgan sent one to fetch José from his yucca patch. A small girl offered a pineapple and Joaquín sliced off the skin with his machete and handed it to Page, a great lollipop of fruit with the stem left on as a handle.

She came over to offer Morgan a bite. "Couldn't Joaquín get us to the Autana as well as José? He seems like a good man too."

"He doesn't know the region like José. We have to follow four rivers to get there. We go on up the Maraviare a ways more and then we have to turn up the Abapo. But the entrance is hidden by undergrowth and fallen trees and you can't see it."

"José knows where it is?"

"Yes," Morgan paused. "Then from the Abapo we turn into the Siapa and from that into the Marana. That's where the real trouble starts. The jungle around there is permanently flooded. The water's chest deep and there are gullies where you'd sink out of sight. Not even a Makiritare can cut through undergrowth he can't see. A boat's the only answer and José is the only one who knows the line to follow through the trees."

Just then José came limping through the door on his stiff right leg. The leg had been crushed years ago when a big *curiara* had overturned in rapids. He had the slight build of the Piaroa tribe and a wizened face that made it difficult not to think of him as an old man. Except for his black hair he looked sixty but he was only forty-one. When he saw Morgan he broke into a smile of recognition, showing half a dozen loose yellow teeth.

"*Hola, amigo.*" Morgan went up to him and they touched each other on the shoulder. With a man like José it was better not to make a fuss. He got right down to business.

"We'd like you to take us to the Autana and wait at the river to bring us back."

"How long?" José asked.

"Three, maybe four days."

"Pay?"

"Twenty bolivars a day and an extra day as bonus." Twenty bolivars was worth about five dollars.

From the gleam in the old man's eyes Morgan knew what question was coming next. "And how much food have you got . . . this time?" The stubby teeth cackled silently.

Morgan laughed. "Enough for eight days."

"*Bueno.*"

That settled it. José limped to where his hammock was hanging, took it down and rolled it up. He found an old khaki shirt mended a dozen times, his machete and a heavy ax with a straight haft four feet long. He spoke a word to the child and limped through the door and down to the river.

"You see that?" Morgan said. "A man of substance with a family and a plot of fruit trees and yucca and he's ready to go in two minutes flat."

"And that medieval ax? He's going to cut through the jungle with it?"

"Not the jungle. The river. You'll see."

In another hour it was lunchtime. Morgan skimmed a thick green froth off the water in the cooking pot and stirred it with a stick. The belly scales, a paler green after the long stewing, rose and sank with the white wedges of flesh still attached. He sucked at the stick and smacked his lips, assembled six tin mugs and doled it out: caiman stew.

Page accepted her mug with a weak smile and Morgan handed her a slice of cassava with a square lump of alligator on top.

"It's firm, dry meat like turtle," he said.

He was watching her. Let's see if she handles the dead one as well as she handled the live. Then we'll go on to the next test.

Page looked at the meat. Nibbled, took a bite and chewed. She dug a piece out of her mug.

"Hey, this isn't bad."

Morgan was pleased. Now for the big one.

"I'm glad you have something solid in you," he said, "because you're about to get your first climbing lesson."

It was more like a final examination than a lesson, he knew. If she's one of these uncoordinated, jelly-kneed bodies on the rock, we've had it.

He opened a pack and began pulling equipment out. "Two miles upriver there's a fifty-foot cliff rising straight out of the water. An hour's practice on it and you'll waltz up the Autana."

Or we'll be back in the *curiara* paddling home.

Page wasn't taken in by Morgan's encouragement. She knew she was on trial.

Before long, after listening carefully to his explanations of climbing technique at the bottom of the cliff, she found herself spread-eagled on it, thirty feet up. Her boots were on two small holds in the rock and her fingertips clutched two more. She felt the gentle tug of the rope leading from her harness up to Morgan, who was standing on a ledge above her tied to a piton he had hammered into a crack. This was what he had told her was called a belay: a point to which the rope or the climber could be attached for safety. A tree or spike of rock would provide a natural belay.

She forced herself to concentrate on his instructions. Take it easy. Don't tense up. She relaxed her fingers and the muscles of her legs until she was perched on her holds without strain. She smiled up at Morgan and then glanced down between her feet at the river where Joaquín, José and the two brothers were watching.

Suddenly Morgan said, "Drop off. Let go."

"But . . ."

"Do as I say. Let go with your hands."

Page took her hands off the rock and fell back into space . . . about one foot. She swung free, her harness taking her weight comfortably.

"Get back on the rock and come up to me."

When she reached him they reversed roles. She tied into the belay piton, took his rope and Morgan climbed down ten feet. He gave a squawk of terror and dropped off. Page felt the strain of his weight through the rope across her back and was amazed at how easily she could hold him.

"Are you confident now that you can fall off any time you want, or don't want, and nothing will happen to you?"

"Yes, it's not so bad if you know someone's going to hold you."

"Good, now that you know how to get up a rock face, I'm going to show you how to get down."

He slung the rope around a tree growing on the edge of the cliff and let the ends dangle down into the water. "You're going to learn what climbers call a rappel. It's a way of walking backwards down a wall." He explained the method. "The rope runs down from the belay tree to your right hand, like this. Then it runs over a brake bar in a carabiner on your harness and across your hip to your left hand, like this. Your left hand controls your speed of descent by increasing or decreasing the friction of the rope against your hip and over the brake bar. Watch, I'll go first."

She watched Morgan walk down the cliff to the bottom and climb back up to her. "Your turn," he said.

Page leaned back over the drop and found she could stop simply by pulling with her left hand. She eased off a little and started down. It was an airy and exciting experience, and she laughed aloud.

Morgan slid down after her with an approving grin and took two metal devices from the pack.

"One more lesson and you're ready," he said. "When we're on the Autana there'll be places where it'll be quicker for you to follow me up the rope instead of climbing the rock. You can't possibly pull yourself up this thin rope hand over hand, so climbers invented these devices called jumars."

He clipped one onto the rope. "See how they hook onto the rope when you put downward pressure on them? But you can slide them up easily. You put your feet in these loops attached to them and you can go up the rope by pushing them up step by step."

After a few flailing attempts Page got the hang of it. She climbed to the top of the cliff and then rappelled down. Morgan climbed up halfway and met her on the ledge.

"My God, David, this is fun."

"You did very well. Not many people get the hang of it so quickly."

"Can I get up the Autana?" It was the crucial question.

"I think you'll make it," he told her.

Page's view of Morgan had undergone several changes. She had known him first only from the pictures of him in his book and as a voice, the intelligent droll observer of his prose style. Under the circumstances their initial meeting had come as a terrible disappointment to her. But now she was beginning to see him as neither a celebrity nor an ogre. A real person, and a rare teacher who had just introduced her, gently and patiently, to a new world.

She looked down and saw that Joaquín and the others were busy filling the outboard gasoline tank from the big drum. Without warning she put her arms around Morgan and kissed him.

"Careful," he said. Holding onto the piton with one hand he pulled her to him. "You're not tied on."

"Then hold me," she said.

He grinned, clipped his harness into the piton and put both arms around her.

"You're held."

Page eyed the piton warily. "Is that safe? Can it hold us?"

"Sure."

"Could climbers make love on a rock wall?"

Morgan laughed. "No such luck. I'm afraid getting up the Autana is going to be too tough for fun and games on the belays."

As they rounded a bend several miles farther upriver she saw what he meant. In the distance, leaning slightly to one side and shimmering in heat haze, a great monolith of red-and-yellow sandstone soared two thousand feet out of the jungle. Its skyward thrust was more than arrogant, it was sublime. Page was ready to believe that nothing in the world was bigger. Certainly nothing was more abrupt. There was no gradation, no graceful curve of flanks leading to an ethereal summit. It rose as plug-ugly from the jungle as a fire hydrant from the pavement. Straight up from the deep green forest to the line of grass and trees on its flat top. It was El Autana.

She gripped the side of the *curiara*. "My God, we're going to climb that!"

Morgan had studied it before from this point. With a strong team he would be ready to use expansion bolts and hammer his way up those vast blank walls directly to the cave. But not with Page.

"See that left-hand edge? That's the north ridge. It's our way up. We'll climb to the top and then cross over to above the cave and rappel down to it."

He saw her studying the knife-blade ridge and sensed her fear. If there was one thing worse than climbing with a beginner it was climbing with a frightened beginner.

"It won't be so bad. See those two notches? They look tiny but they're probably big ledges. They'll give us a rest."

"But it's so sheer."

"If there are holds, you can climb it the same way you climb a ladder."

"What holds? It looks as smooth as concrete."

"Wait till you're close up. That ridge is twice as high as the Empire State Building. The crack above the second step is twenty stories high. The red slab on the right is as big as three football fields."

The *curiara* turned and the mountain vanished behind the trees.

At the next bend it loomed into view again from a different angle. Three-quarters of the way up in the center was a bright pinhead of light shining through the mountain.

Page reached for her camera. "Look, there's the cave. The Eye of the Gods."

"I've seen it before and I still find it hard to believe," Morgan said. "You realize that little speck of light is probably big enough to fly a small plane through if you could find a pilot nutty enough to try it."

Page caught sight of a line of smaller openings running along the face at the same level. "What about those other caves?"

"I noticed them last time. They're dark so they don't go all the way through. They probably open into galleries. There must be a whole system of tunnels and chambers up there."

"How many rappels will it take to get down?" she said.

"About four."

She looked worried. "I wonder what it feels like going over the edge with two thousand feet of nothing below you."

"It's what climbers call sensational," he said. In other words, he thought, it scares the hell out of you. "Just come down at a steady pace. The friction of the rope through the carabiner will make it very hot. If you stop it may start melting the nylon rope. So don't rush and don't stop."

"Now he tells me."

"You've rappelled down a fifty-foot wall. There's no difference in technique for a two thousand-foot wall."

"How do we get back down to the bottom of the mountain?"

"Same way. We'll rappel down from the cave."

As the *curiara* came out of the bend the angle changed and the point of light flickered out. Now there was only the awesome wall, waiting for them in the distance.

José, hunched under his wide-brimmed hat in the bow, moved for the first time in two hours. Without looking back he raised his left arm and pointed to the bank. It was the hidden entrance to the Abapo.

Joaquín turned the *curiara* and headed toward the apparently unbroken jungle. When they reached it José attacked the branches and lianas with his machete while the other men pulled the boat through, a yard at a time. Soon they entered a black creek winding between walls of vegetation at times only ten feet apart and meeting overhead.

José was giving two signs now, one to show the direction of the next bend, the other to show whether to accelerate or slow down. Joaquín picked it up, surging around the bends. Every few minutes the whole crew would duck as low-hanging branches came at them splintering against the *curiara* and showering them with clouds of stinging ants.

From time to time there would be a yell of warning and Joaquín would cut the motor as they ran headlong onto a fallen tree. The *curiara* was designed for this. It would run up onto the trunk and either push it down and pass over or break through with its weight. But at times it jammed on top and the crew would have to heave it over. Everyone except Page would get out onto the trunk and heave while José chanted the timing, *ún, dos, ún, dos.*

Once they ran onto a huge tree that wouldn't give, and now Page saw what the ax was for. José hefted it and in half an hour cut through the wood. The operation was like clearing a fallen tree from a narrow road. The difference was that there were fifteen or twenty feet of water beneath them with God knows what lurking beneath it. This didn't seem to bother the brothers. Page had begun to think of them as a vaudeville act: the Laughing Hyenas. Each obstacle was met with howls of laughter. The worse the problem, the wilder the cackles. If we sink they'll split their sides, she thought.

The next time they ran onto a solid trunk José decided to lighten ship before they heaved it over. The packs were handed out and hung on the branches. Page saw one slip off and sink.

"Hey, David," she called, then realized what the pack contained and changed her mind. Morgan looked back and she shook her head. "Nothing. It's okay."

But as the *curiara* slid over the tree and moved on she looked back at where the pack had sunk out of sight.

My God, Foster, she thought, you don't even know if two people can fit in a single bat tent.

They emerged from the flooded area and followed the upper course of the Marana for five miles until the way was blocked by rapids. José waved them into the bank. The river journey was over but they still had a long march through the jungle to the foot of the mountain.

Morgan conferred with Joaquín and turned to Page. "We'll start with José and take the bivouac and climbing equipment. Joaquín and the boys will follow with the other stuff."

José picked up his machete and hesitated with his back to the river. He seemed to be relying on some sixth sense rather than looking or listening. Morgan weighed the odds against him. He hadn't seen the Autana for over an hour and since then the river had changed direction constantly. He couldn't see it now because it was several miles away and the dense tangle cut visibility to a few yards. Even with clear skies it was often difficult to place the sun, the Indians' compass, because of the foliage overhead. Now clouds had sailed in. Which direction to take? Abruptly José struck off into the undergrowth ahead of him.

The floor of the jungle became fairly clear but the terrain remained rugged. There were rocky stretches and crevices concealed by humus and leaves. Before long they were streaming with sweat. It started under the packs on their backs and spread until every inch of clothing was soaked.

José moved quickly, taking the easiest line around obstacles, changing direction dozens of times until it was impossible to guess where the river was. Morgan notched trees at intervals, cutting a blaze on the forward side to guide them on their way back. José's method was subtler: a deft nick in thin saplings so that they fell over at right angles away from the trail without being severed. This was a clear pointer whether you were coming or going along the trail.

Morgan stopped at a rotting tree and picked up a stick. "Watch this." He jabbed the tree and in an instant big red ants were swarming up the stick. He dropped it. "They're fire ants. Their sting is fierce so watch what you grab onto when you're climbing a slope."

He picked a big gray fly off Page's shoulder and showed it to her. "These are *tabanos.* You can't just wave them away. You have to smack them off."

"Any other interesting creatures?"

"As I said, it's the small beasts who rule around here. No Cuyakiares."

The ground was rising and the ups and downs grew steeper. As Morgan reached the top of the next rise he found José standing at the edge of a clearing pointing upward. Towering unbelievably high above them was the Autana. Right on target. Morgan slapped him on the shoulder.

He studied the first stretch of the ridge. Two hundred feet to a tree and a resting place followed by a pinnacle and one hundred fifty feet of vegetated wall, steep but feasible. Then the first major problem, a long line of overhangs cutting across the face. He picked out a route through them: an overhanging crack, a steep slab, then a rising traverse to a sensational jutting nose. Beyond that point the wall rose dizzily and he made no attempt to decipher it. One problem at a time.

Page stood beside him. "Do you still think I can make it?" she said.

"Sure," Morgan said. "If anyone can."

It took him a moment to realize that this time he meant it, he wasn't simply trying to boost her morale. They had started off through the jungle again and he stopped and looked at her as if seeing her for the first time.

"What's wrong?" she said.

"Nothing," he said. "Nothing at all."

They went on and Morgan was thinking that he had just made an extraordinary discovery.

9

In an hour they were close to the foot of the mountain and shortly afterward Joaquín and the brothers arrived and a camp took shape. Twenty-foot saplings were cut and tied with lianas in two triangles to support a roof pole. A tarpaulin was flung over this and the hammocks were slung from cross-poles on each side. The fact that their campsite was on a slope that was only forty degrees from the vertical, Page noted, was apparently no impediment to Makiritare engineering skill.

"It would take Himalayan Sherpas to match them," Morgan told her.

He began to build a fire. "Joaquín's going dove hunting to liven up our beans and rice. It's dusk. The birds will be heading for the river to drink. Why don't you go with him?"

"I'd love to. But what's he going to use? He hasn't got a gun."

"He doesn't need one. He's got his blowpipe."

"That should be something."

Joaquín was waiting for her and they started off. Walking behind him Page had a hard time keeping her eyes off the lean muscular buttocks on either side of his faded red *guayuco*. She caught up with him, pointing in sign language.

"Shoot? Birds?"

He faced her amiably but said nothing.

"Me Tarzan, you Jane," she said and fell in behind him again, smiling to herself as they continued on.

They were heading for a small stream that Morgan had told her was nearby. Soon, Joaquín using his machete to clear a path, they came into the open and the stream was before them, a good fifteen yards wide but shallow enough to wade across. Page followed him down the muddy bank and out onto a sandy spit.

"Is this where we hunt?"

He raised his fingers to his lips.

"Sorry," she said, "I forgot you're the strong, silent type."

With his hand still raised he scanned the sky, pale blue and tinged with sunset, opening up between the trees.. She saw birds flickering back and forth over the stream. Joaquín's face, set off by his basin-cropped hair, was intent. Primitive but handsome. He was wearing a string of clawlike teeth around his neck.

He took a white-feathered dart from the pouch at his side and inserted it in the mouthpiece of his blowpipe. She stepped back to give him room and he raised the blowpipe to his lips, holding it with both hands around the mouthpiece in a distinctive grip, one hand beneath to support it, the other above to steady, one elbow pointing down, the other out to the side.

He held the blowpipe raised toward the birds flickering back and forth against the sky like cinders. Then Page saw him swing it. She didn't see the dart leave it any more than she would see buckshot leaving a shotgun. She saw one of the cinders suddenly detached from the others, spinning down in an arc with the white feather attached to it and hitting the water with a plop.

"My God, what a shot!"

Joaquín received the compliment stolidly. He waited for the current to carry the white feather to them. When it came up he waded out and retrieved it. The bird was a mourning dove, bluish-gray with a whitish underbelly, a bead of blood on its black beak. He removed the dart and tossed the bird on the sand at their feet, reinserted the dart and repeated the performance.

After a few more shots he let Page try. The blowpipe was light enough for a child to lift. She hesitated considering the possibility of contracting a rare tropical disease, then placed her lips to the slightly moist end. Blowing as hard as she could while at the same time trying to swing the blowpipe she saw the white feather fly a few feeble yards before dropping birdless in the water.

"I'll let you do the hunting from now on."

Joaquín went back to work and by the time it was getting dark he had collected about a dozen doves. He squatted and put them in a burlap sack and rose with the sack and his blowpipe.

"You know, you're really something," Page said, unable to resist teasing him.

He turned to face her.

"So maybe you're not much of a talker but what the hell, nobody's perfect."

She started back to camp ahead of him feeling very pleased with herself. All at once Joaquín spoke.

She whirled. "What!"

He said nothing. She peered at him in the fading light.

"Did you just say something?"

If he had he wasn't about to admit it. Page felt embarrassed. She had probably imagined it.

Funny, though, she thought, it had sounded as if he were returning the compliment in French.

Back in camp the fire was going and Morgan was warming up their beans and rice in the pot he had used for lunch. Joaquín tossed his sack to one of the brothers, who went off with it.

"How was your hunt?" Morgan asked her.

"Wonderful. It's amazing the way he can do it. When I read about it in your book I didn't believe it."

"Really? You seemed to believe everything else."

Page laughed, flopping down beside him. "You've got me there."

José, looking more grizzled than ever, was drinking from a bottle.

"It's the native brew," Morgan told her. "Want some?"

She considered the bottle and the drinker. "I think I'll pass. I wouldn't want to end up looking sixty when I'm forty-one. Thirty's bad enough."

Joaquín appeared with six improvised spits, branches he had hacked off and trimmed, and he and Morgan spoke in Spanish, laughing conspiratorially.

"What's so funny?" Page said.

"He says he enjoyed hunting with you."

The brother returned with the doves plucked, gutted and washed on the burlap sack.

"Ready for dinner?" Morgan said.

"You bet. I'm famished."

He skewered a dove and handed her the spit. Tin plates of beans and rice were passed out.

After a while he said, "Yours looks about done."

She removed the bird and holding it in both hands, bit into it. "Mm, these are good. How about another?"

"Celestino," Morgan said to the brother who had prepared the birds, *"otra paloma, por favor."*

Page held her spit out and the brother fixed a dove on it. They sat eating and talking.

"This has been a marvelous day," she said.

Morgan seemed momentarily preoccupied. "Yes, you did quite well."

"I'm sorry I made you come," Page said. "I never would have been able to do it without you."

"Don't be silly. You didn't make me anyway, my paper did. I'm looking forward to it as much as you are, now that we're here."

"Then what's wrong?"

"Oh, nothing. I was just thinking of Mabruk."

"Didn't you say the ransom demand would be met? Then they'll release him, right?"

"They should, if they're professionals. But you never can tell. They seemed professional. Anyone who could pull off a job like that."

"You went to school with him?" Page said.

"Mabruk? Yes. We didn't see all that much of each other but we were friendly enough, and we've been in contact off and on since then."

"What's he like?"

"He's a good fellow. Nobody ever thought he would turn out the way he has. He was sort of a frivolous character at Cambridge, running around without any responsibilities to speak of. But when he became the heir to the throne he took hold."

"How did he become the heir?"

"The King's only son died in an airplane crash a year or so after we got out of university. When the King named Mabruk his successor, everyone said it wouldn't work. There were people in the council who were violently opposed to it. Still are for that matter. But he's fooled them. He'll make a good ruler . . . if he lives."

Morgan was gloomy again and Page decided to change the subject. Joaquín was conversing with José and the two brothers.

"You see," she said, "I knew he could talk. I couldn't get him to say a word while we were hunting."

Morgan cheered up. "He's something of a put-on artist. Was he doing his wooden Indian routine?"

"Deaf and dumb is more like it."

"Mira, amigo," Morgan said to Joaquín. They spoke together laughing.

"What's he say?"

"He says you were doing so much talking he couldn't get a word in edgewise."

"Well I suppose I was going on a bit."

"Nonsense," Joaquín suddenly said to her in English. "You were very amusing."

Page looked startled. Joaquín and Morgan were grinning.

"It's about time," Morgan said to him. "I was getting a little tired of this."

"That makes two of us," Joaquín said.

"Hey wait a minute!" Page said. "What is this!"

"I'm afraid he's been having a little fun with you."

She peered at Joaquín. "You mean you speak English!"

"Now and then," he said.

The two men were laughing. "Very funny," she said.

"Don't feel bad," Morgan said. "He did the same thing to me when I first met him."

"But how come you speak English?" she asked.

Joaquín shrugged as if the answer were simple. "My mother was an American and my father was a Makiritare."

But the answer really wasn't so simple. The brothers had risen and collected the tin plates and utensils and gone off to wash them. José sat drinking from his bottle. Joaquín looked across the fire at Page. He enjoyed his life as a Makiritare and his freedom to travel without being a subject of gossip, and he wanted to keep it that way. But Morgan was his friend and he liked this woman.

"Have you ever heard of Amy Erickson?" he asked her.

"The flyer, the one who disappeared years ago?" Page said.

"She didn't really disappear. She crash-landed on that little landing strip where you and David came down yesterday. It was in even worse shape in 1938 than it is today."

"I thought she was never heard from again."

"She wasn't," Joaquín said. "When she met my father she realized this was where she wanted to spend the rest of her life. The only ones who knew were her parents. They weren't too happy about it but they were glad she was alive. I think they were afraid of the scandal if it ever got out that their daughter was married to a Venezuelan Indian chief."

Page gave Morgan a skeptical look. "Is this another of his put-ons?"

"No, it's the truth."

"Then how come you've never published it?"

Morgan made a face as if to say "How come, indeed."

"Friendship," he said. "Joaquín is afraid if the world ever finds out he's the son of Amy Erickson the famous aviator, it'd be the end of the Makiritare. They'd never be left alone and neither would he."

"Actually I'm only here about six months a year," Joaquín told her. "The rest of the time I'm traveling. My grandparents left me pretty well off."

Morgan played an imaginary violin. "Don't you feel sorry for him? You should see him at the blackjack table in Monte Carlo in his white dinner jacket with a beautiful woman on his arm. Makes you weep."

"But this is my home," Joaquín said. "It was where I was born and raised. The Makiritare are the greatest hunters in the world. Sometimes we go off for weeks, men, women and children. We camp out and hunt every day and eat what we kill. Deer, jaguar, tapir . . . You see these teeth around my neck? They're peccary tusks."

"Have you ever seen Cuyakiare?" she asked.

He shook his head. "I'm afraid not. I hate to say it, but I think you're kidding yourself."

"She's been victimized by reading my book," Morgan said.

"I'm beginning to feel you're right," Page said.

"Don't take our word for it," Joaquín said. "José here has seen Cuyakiare plenty of times if you care to believe him."

José looked up from his bottle and Joaquín spoke to him. Instantly the old man grew animated and began to tell a story. Joaquín translated.

"He says he once saw Cuyakiare stick his head out the cave on the Autana and it filled the whole opening. He could even see his teeth, they were that big.

"Another time he was hunting with his dogs and all of a sudden they began to howl and race off on a scent."

"Ah-ooo! Ah-ooo!" José imitated his pack.

"He ran after them thinking they must have treed a jaguar. Then there was a roar and the ground began to shake and all the dogs came running back."

José gestured vigorously, slurring his words between the stubs of his few teeth.

"He says Cuyakiare appeared and he shot at him with his blowpipe and then ran like hell."

The story ended abruptly with a fatalistic shrug.

"He was so scared he wasn't able to climb on his wife for a month. Which isn't surprising if you've ever seen his wife," Joaquín added.

Page began to laugh. "Morgan why didn't you tell me your so-called eyewitnesses sounded so ridiculous."

"I tried to. But you weren't in any mood to listen."

She lay with her head in his lap, watching the play of shadows and firelight in the dark foliage above.

"Well, at least it'll be fun to see what it's like up in the cave," she said.

"That's true," Morgan agreed.

He added to himself, *If* we can get up.

10

The crack in the rock was overhanging, green with moss, oozing with water. They had struggled up a crumbling gully to reach it. Now sheer walls rose on either side. Page pouted at the evil-looking fissure.

"Is that what you call a breach in the ramparts?"

"It's the only breach there is," Morgan said, "but it's not as bad as it looks. What worries me is that big overhang four hundred feet up. That's going to be a real bastard."

She grimaced at Joaquín, who had carried one of their two climbing packs. "That's all he's talked about since we got up this morning. The overhang."

"He's just working himself up for it, that's all."

"And the first step," Morgan said, "is to see we've got our kit on right."

He examined the bowlines that tied the red and white climbing ropes into the carabiner on Page's harness. Then turned her around and ran his hands over the webbing on her back and shoulders. Finally he checked his climbing kit: hammer, pitons, slings.

"Okay, now listen. I'll go up the crack about twenty feet and traverse left onto the face and continue on up. When I reach a decent ledge, clip the packs onto the white rope and shout "Up pack" for each one. Got it?"

"Right."

"After I haul the packs," he told her, "you jumar up this red rope, which I'll belay above. Use your hammer to bash out any pitons you come to because we'll need them farther up. When you get to the top retrieve the rope and follow me up the ridge."

"All on my own?"

"Yes, dummy."

He slapped Joaquín on the shoulder, turned and attacked the corner. His first foothold broke off under his boot. His left handhold crumbled into yellow paste. Falling, he slithered down the gully a few feet.

"Rock's as soft as soap," he said and attacked once more.

Reaching high he jammed his hand in the crack, pulled up and whipped in another jam. One more heave and he was able to grab a good hold and pull up until he was bridged across the corner twenty feet up. He made these moves in one continuous sequence and Page felt her spirits lift out of the funk produced by the spectacle of her guide falling off the first six feet of the mountain.

But the guide was in top form. He moved left onto the wall and climbed out of sight.

"He's really going," she said.

Joaquín nodded. "I've heard other climbers say he's a natural. He's very strong for his weight."

The rope stopped moving upward and they heard Morgan's voice above.

"On belay. Ready to haul."

Page clipped the first pack onto the rope. "Up pack," she called in a surprisingly powerful mezzo-soprano and the heavy duffel bag shot up the first three feet of its journey. Soon the rope snaked down the wall again and the second pack went up. Now it was Page's turn.

"Well, here goes. So long."

"Good luck," Joaquín said, "and don't worry about that overhang. He'll get you over it."

Page clipped the jumars on the rope, put her feet into the nylon loops and started up. Twenty feet up she began to gain confidence. She had the right rhythm with the jumars and she was ascending a wall she couldn't possibly climb otherwise. Glancing behind her she saw she was already above the trees and felt relieved to be out of the claustrophobic green shadows. She glanced down for her last view of the blurred upturned face of Joaquín, now seventy feet below, and then up for her first sight of Morgan perched on a ledge fifty feet above her.

Left jumar up, stand in loop, right jumar up, stand in loop, left jumar . . .

She reached a piton that Morgan had hammered into a crack to give him protection on his way up. She braced her feet against the rock, unsheathed her hammer and worked the peg out of the crack with alternate blows from left and right. Clipping it into a carabiner on her harness, she grabbed the jumars and started up, reveling in her competence. She glanced down and estimated the height. It had been ninety feet before Morgan had needed the piton. He must be climbing like a demon.

She was still trying to cook up a jaunty greeting when she reached his belay ledge and found him gone, and the packs too. Level with her head was the end of the white rope, and leaning out she could see it running up over a series of short walls. I can manage that okay, she thought. I'll use one jumar as a handhold and scramble up.

She turned outward on the narrow ledge and gasped with delight. There was a vast expanse of jungle below, rolling away fifteen miles to rise in a mountain with white waterfalls spilling down it and a rainbow arching over it through bronze clouds. On her right the sun shone straight into her eyes, but below her the gully was still in shadows.

Page was conscious that she had gone through a barrier. She had passed from the horizontal world to the vertical.

A hundred feet farther up she found Morgan sprawled on a ledge, disheveled, sweating and out of breath. She was startled at the contrast with her own fresh feeling but she soon understood the reason: the two packs sitting next to him. With the plastic ten-liter water tank they weighed fifty pounds each.

Page considered what it was like to pick up a fifty-pound suitcase and translated it into terms of pack hauling. You stand on a ledge, reach down, grasp the rope and heave up the fifty pounds, hold it with one hand, reach down with the other and heave again. Repeat the process fifty or sixty times, heaving with both hands and all your guts when the pack jams under an overhang, and finally wrestle it onto the ledge and tie it to your belay or heave it above your head to clip into a piton. And that's just the first pack. By the time you were done, you would have to peel your fingers from the rope.

She watched him kneading his hands and wincing. He was looking upward. She looked too. My God, she thought, that overhang *is* big. Morgan had called it a roof and that's exactly what it was. Get under it and you'd sure have a roof over your head, about eight feet of it sticking straight out. Except that when you get to the outer edge the wall continues straight up again.

The overhang ran across the face and there was no way around it. To get over it Morgan would have to crawl out under it like a fly upside down on a ceiling.

She looked at him. "How in hell do we climb that?"

"See that crack thirty feet below it? That's the jump-off point. I'll climb up to it and hammer in two pitons, one for the packs and one for the belay. When you come up you'll have to hang from the belay and pay out my rope as I go over the roof. *If* I go over it, that is."

"You better get some fuel in you first," Page said, opening the ration pack. "What'll you have, chocolate, raisins?"

"No, give me the mixture. It's like spinach for Popeye," he grinned.

She passed him a plastic tube containing his personal concoction of wheat germ, honey and condensed milk. He squeezed out two mouthfuls without taking his eyes off the overhang. Page took her share and they both had a swig from the water bottle. Lunch was over.

Morgan checked his equipment and climbed one hundred fifty feet to the crack. He hammered in the pitons and hauled the packs, clipping them into the lower one. Page followed and clipped into the upper. Hanging from it she took the rope and nodded to him.

"Good luck."

He climbed thirty feet until he was directly under the roof. He moved to the right and hammered a piton in. From this point a crack cut across the roof to its outer edge. He could move out along that crack.

Clipping his rope into the piton and using a sling for support he leaned out and back and drove a piton upward into the roof halfway to the outer edge. He took an étrier from his belt and clipped it to the piton. The étrier was a length of webbing with sewn-in loops for the feet that a climber could stand in when there were no holds in the rock. Morgan clipped his rope into the piton and hitching his boot up into one of the loops he swung under the roof. Now with one foot doubled under him and the other stretched full-length, he reached out and back once more to drive another peg into the roof crack almost at the edge. He was horizontal in space beneath the overhang: a human fly. Clipping in another étrier he stepped into it, reached over the overhang for a hold and stood up with a violent swing. He reached up with his other hand and whooped with triumph.

"There's a jug! A bloody great jug! We've cracked it!"

A 'jug,' Page remembered, was short for 'jug handle,' which in climbers' argot is a good handhold you can curl your fingers around. With that sort of aid she could crack it too.

Morgan had retrieved the étriers before vanishing over the overhang, and the ropes hung down to her. This meant she was expected to jumar up the free-swinging rope, in thin air, until she reached the jug above the roof and was able to pull herself up and over.

As she unclipped the packs and watched them jerking up, she steeled herself, running through the instructions Morgan had given her. Above all, keep your balance. Don't fall backward so your feet shoot out in front and you have to struggle to force yourself upright again. Keep your feet under your body and your chin up so you can touch the rope with it.

The last pack went up and Page was ready. She glanced down at the trees four hundred feet below, unclipped the jumars from her harness, fixed them on the rope and with a muttered prayer, started up. For the first twelve feet the rope hung down against the face and she had no trouble. Then the rock fell back and the rope rose straight up to the edge of the overhang, twenty feet above.

That's just two stories high, she told herself. Nothing to it. She moved up away from the rock and instantly began to twirl. The horizon spun round and as she faced outward she gasped at the sudden exposure. Then she was facing in and the rock spun dizzily across her line of vision. She shut her eyes and felt the glare of the sun on them as the spin faced her outward again.

Her hands were gripping the jumars so tightly they hurt. Relax, she told herself, don't tense up or you'll exhaust yourself. Morgan had said there was no way to stop the spinning. She just had to grit her teeth and keep going.

Morgan's voice called down. "You coming?"

Page took a deep breath to calm her thudding heart.

She started up the rope. By the time she reached the jug she was beginning to smile. When she got up to Morgan, thirty feet above the overhang, she was boasting.

"Piece of cake, as you Limeys say."

The next two hundred fifty feet were climbed quickly. The rock was steep but there were holds and several generous ledges that gave Morgan a good stance for hauling the packs. On one straightforward pitch of fifty feet Page hitched one of the packs to her harness and despite Morgan's protests jumared up with it hanging from her. It was hard work but she was glad to relieve him of one of the loads.

They arrived at last on the first major notch in the ridge. As Morgan had predicted, it was big. He sized up the rock above. The prow of the ridge was split by a chimney, which was a crack wide enough to let the climber get inside. Above that was a steep, vegetated section of about seventy feet and then a forty-foot wall. Beyond, the ridge was invisible, which meant that with a bit of luck, it fell back from the vertical. He saw no major problem to that point.

Behind him he found Page with her arms stretched out to the west, one closed fist above the other.

"Are you okay, miss?" he asked.

"Sunset is at seven. There's three fists and a finger between the sun and the horizon. At one hour a fist that means the time is ten of four."

Morgan grinned. She sounded as confident as the Greenwich Observatory. He pulled out his watch and swallowed.

"Well?" she said.

"Well. It's ten minutes to four."

They sat down laughing and Page pounded him derisively in the chest. She had the advantage and was determined to press it. She looked around at the ledge with disfavor. There was ample room to spread out two separate sleeping bags and that wasn't her idea at all. She hadn't let one of their bat tents sink out of sight for nothing. She turned to Morgan.

"We're not going to stop here, are we, so early in the day?"

He looked at her with approval. "You're not tired? Good for you. You're right. The proper thing is to press on while the weather holds and the rock is dry."

He stood up and pulled her to her feet. "Anyway we're not on a damned picnic. We're out to snare a dinosaur."

They dragged the packs over to the bottom of the chimney and Morgan climbed it, hauled the packs and went on, while Page jumared up the face to the left of the chimney on the red rope.

They kept at it, hardly needing to exchange a word when they met at belays and going so fast that before Morgan knew it they were in trouble. In the last hour the ridge had steepened. There were no longer any ledges for stances, let alone a bivouac. He was a hundred feet above Page. He had managed to get his first good piton in but couldn't figure out his next move over the bulge above him. In the failing light he probed with a piton at arm's length and miraculously slotted it into a crack he couldn't see. He drove it in with his hammer and listened approvingly as the blows echoed with a rising, singing ping, the signal that a piton is going in solid and true.

He glanced down at Page. Below her for a hundred and fifty feet there was nothing remotely resembling a decent ledge to spend the night on. Morgan considered his pitons and the bulge above them and came to a decision. They would spend the night in the bat tents.

He called to Page to clip the packs on. He hauled them up and clipped them to the lower piton. As she jumared up he rummaged in the personal-kit pack and got a bat tent. He shook it out, rigged its roof and clipped it to the upper piton, calculating the distance so that the second tent would hang close beneath it without touching the rock or needing a roof of its own.

Page reached him and began to hold forth about their situation, which she called "extraterrestrial." It was, too. They were looking down at the sun as it slipped below the horizon with one last flash of gold on some far-off river. Beneath and all around them was darkening space. On their left, to the east, the sky was black, with clear bright stars beginning to glow.

Morgan listened in surprise as she chattered on. They were, after all, hanging from pitons over one thousand feet of empty air. Come to think of it, she was more than nonchalant. She was flip, as if putting up a front. Maybe she's scared, he thought.

He was still rummaging in the pack, and beginning to grumble.

"I can't find that other damned bat tent. Could it be in the food pack?"

"No, it couldn't," Page said flatly.

"How do you know?"

"Because it's at the bottom of the river. I saw it sink."

"You what! When? Where for God's sake?"

"When we unloaded to get over that big tree trunk."

"And you let it go?"

"Yes."

"What in God's name for?"

Page's eyes were very steady on his. "You really mean you don't know?"

"No. I don't."

"You're slow today. Well, I'll tell you and you'd better get used to it. You've got a woman in your bat tent tonight."

Morgan stared at her. Then he grinned. Then they were both laughing like lunatics.

"You know, the idea of making love in a bat tent crossed my mind down in the village," he said. "But it was only an idea. You went ahead and did something about it." He pulled her to him and kissed her. "That must be what's known as Yankee know-how."

Without another word Page struggled into the bat tent and took off her harness. Her clothes followed. First boots, then socks. Then her shirt, blue jeans, bra and panties. It was a slow strip because each item had to be safely secured before the next came off. Morgan didn't mind a bit.

Naked at last, she leaned back in the yielding position that was the only one the hammock permitted. There was a scent of warm skin in that wilderness of rock and air. Morgan saw her curved thighs in the fading light. Gentle fingers ranged over her body and his mouth brushed down from her throat to her breasts. Then, naked too, he eased under the canopy.

Immediately the preliminaries ceased. There was only one position for two people in a bat tent. Page described the maneuver afterward: Don't knock, come right in. But I mean right in.

It was full moonlight before a low laugh sounded from the bat tent and a spectral figure emerged, tied itself to a piton and pulled on its pants. Shortly afterward two slim legs were raised and a pair of panties slipped over them to be drawn on by their wriggling owner.

"Watch it," Morgan said, grabbing the hammock to steady it. "You'll tip yourself out. Get your harness on."

Page was radiant but still the practical woman. "Gotta eat," she said.

They rummaged around and soon a flashlight was attached to the upper piton. Chocolate and biscuits, raisins and cheese appeared, and Morgan mixed cold instant tea in his water bottle. He sat easily in his harness, food in his lap, the plastic tea bottle between his knees. Page leaned back happily in the hammock, her hands full of goodies.

"Even Batso wouldn't believe it," she said.

"He might, just."

"It's romantic. It's wild. It's outta sight. I always dreamed of an adventure. But I never thought it would be like this."

"You mean danger or love?"

"I suppose a bit of both."

"Didn't you ever have a love adventure?"

Page shrugged. "John isn't exactly the adventurous type. I've been going with him for five years. He's in banking. At least he's dependable."

"You depend on him?"

"I guess so." She looked at him surprised. "The way you ask sounds as though you don't like the idea."

Morgan didn't answer. He was thinking, I believe you're right.

Page sat up in the bat tent. "My God, he's human. Our roving adventurer has a heart. And it's been smitten by me."

He grinned. "Any more of that talk and I'll have your pants off."

There was a three-second convulsion in the bat tent.

"They're off," she said.

Morgan crawled in and there was another convulsion, longer than three seconds.

It was a sleepy but happy voice that next broke the silence. Page nudged Morgan.

"How's your piton holding out?"

"I beg your pardon."

"I mean the piton we're hanging from."

"Oh, that's okay, it's solidly placed."

"You're pretty confident, aren't you?" She ran her fingers across the two-day stubble on his chin.

"Not any more than you. I've never seen anyone do better than you first time on a mountain."

"I've got a good teacher."

"Thank you, miss."

They were silent a moment.

"Aren't you glad you came?" Page said.

"What, to search for your bloody dinosaur?"

"No, idiot. To climb the Autana."

"I wouldn't have missed it for a gold clock. I admit I got surly when I was pulled off the kidnap story but that's the newsman's curse, always at the mercy of every disaster that comes along. Oh, the noble newsman, bloody vulture feeding off the carrion of events."

Morgan gave her a squeeze. "How about you, aren't you glad you came?"

She squeezed him back. "I wouldn't have missed it either . . . with or without my bloody dinosaur."

They untangled themselves and got out of the bat tent before daybreak. By sunrise their gear was stowed, they had shared a tube of the mixture and Morgan was pulling up over the bulge. They both felt indomitable and climbed nonstop for four hours.

About midmorning Page found Morgan leaning out over the west wall. He came back onto the edge of the ridge and motioned her to lean out too. Puzzled, she swept her eyes over the blank gray expanse.

Then she saw it. A vegetated ledge, a curving arch of rock seen edge-on. It was the cave, level with them but five hundred feet away. Page was trembling with excitement and Morgan had to pull her back.

"It seems close. But we have to get to the top before we can rappel down to it."

"Well, I'm ready. Let's go."

The angle eased on the next section of the ridge but after a hundred feet it reared up in a curious concave wall. Even from below there was something about it Morgan didn't like.

When he got to the wall he saw why. It was bone-dry, yellow, crumbling sandstone: a rotten scab on the firm rock of the ridge. There was a big flake of rock eight feet high, five feet wide, balanced on a ledge. Loose rocks like this were always a danger on an unclimbed ridge. If it fell it would crush Page and drag them both off.

Morgan examined the flake. There was no way around it but he reckoned it must weigh a ton. He could probably climb over it without shifting it. He climbed lightly up the flake until he stood on top of it. From there it was only one step to a ledge above. He made the step but as he pushed up off the flake it heeled out and fell.

The first impact was fifty feet below. It struck the ridge with an appalling bang, a fizz of sparks and a cloud of splinters. It plunged again in total silence toward Page and struck in an explosion of noise and debris. It seemed minutes before the rumbling echoes died and the block, sweeping everything in its path, smashed itself to pieces hundreds of feet down the ridge.

Morgan shouted frantically, "Are you okay? Page, answer me!"

There was no sound. He hammered a piton into a crack, tied his rope to it and started down in a fast rappel.

He reached the huge scar where the flake had struck first. There was that familiar smell in the air like cordite, like exploded bombs. He leaned out to look down. Page was flat against the rock. He shot down to her, passing the livid scar where the flake had struck, three feet above her head. She was covered with dust and rock splinters and her eyes were shut tight.

Morgan would remember her first words forever. Quite quietly she said, "I'm afraid I dropped the piton hammer, Dave . . . what with one thing and another."

Slowly Morgan coaxed her up to where the block had fallen from and then up another fifty feet of easier rock to a small ledge. He looked up, trying to see the top of the mountain, but he couldn't. It might be as much as another three hundred feet up.

He had been thinking of the loss of Page's hammer. He still had his own, but losing one could mean trouble. How much trouble depended on your luck and what sort of obstacles you ran into. The obstacle he was staring up at now was a sobering one.

The ridge had lost its sharp edge, broadening into a buttress that rose a hundred and fifty feet. This was distinguished by a huge boilerplate of rock that overlaid it. The plate was shaped like the west coast of Africa. It ran up seventy-five feet, turned left for thirty feet, and then ran up again to the top. He named it immediately: Africa Plate. The edge of the plate was separated from the main face by a crack two or three inches wide. It was the only line up the otherwise smooth wall.

"You wouldn't believe it," he said, "but we have to climb that crack."

"You do well on cracks, don't you? You can always get a jam hold."

"Yes, but not when they run upside down like that one does halfway up. That has to be climbed with pitons and they have to be hammered in upward, and it really gives you the willies when you put your weight on them."

He squinted. "Come to think of it, that damn crack is too wide for our pitons. I'm afraid it's what we call a stopper."

He began to move about the ledge muttering to himself. Can't get stopped now. We're not bloody well giving up now.

He went to the left and studied the face. Nothing. He crossed to the right and looked up. Nothing. He ran his eye down the right flank of the ridge noting that there was a tree sprouting from a crack fifty feet below. It'd make a good belay for the descent. But wait a moment. A tree. That means wood.

"Wedges!" he shouted, laughing and giving Page a little shake. "That's the answer."

He rummaged in the equipment pack and fished out his heavy knife, rigged a belay and rappelled down to the tree. It was a three-inch-thick sapling. He cut off the top branches, sawed through it, tied the six-foot sapling to his harness and jumared back up to the ledge.

He grinned at Page and stripped off the bark. If this ridge thinks it's going to beat us it's got another thing coming. He cut the sapling into sections six or eight inches long and carved them into wedges. Page had never seen him so worked up. He seethed with a sort of pugnacity. Morgan surveyed his handiwork with satisfaction.

"Right, I think I can get up the straight section without pitons. When I get to the upside-down bit around Nigeria, I'll start hammering these wedges in and then put the pitons in between the wedges and the rock. That's the way they did it in the old days." He was exultant. "There's always a way if you use your . . ."

He stopped as if he'd just remembered he'd left the bath tap running at home. But it wasn't the tap he remembered, it was the piton hammer they'd lost.

"My God, you won't be able to retrieve the pitons. I'll be way over to the left when I reach the top and won't be able to lower my hammer to you."

"You mean we won't have any pitons left for the rest of the climb?"

"Precious few." Morgan became pugnacious again. "But hell with it, we'll get up somehow."

"What about the descent?"

"We'll use bolts."

He put an arm around her shoulders. Page sensed something foreign, almost apologetic in the gesture, as if he were trying to con her and were embarrassed about it.

"There's just one thing," he said. "As I'll be over on the left up there, you're going to have to swing across the rock on the rope until you're underneath me before you start jumaring up."

She looked across the wall. "But that's thirty feet."

"Don't worry. It's what they call a pendulum. Just let your weight come on the rope and run across."

"Run?"

Morgan was full of false assurance. "Nothing to it. You turn your shoulder down toward the jungle and take off. Hundred yard dash and that sort of thing. Be bold about it or you'll scrape across like a sack of potatoes and take the seat out of your pants."

He gave her no chance to protest. "Okay," he said, "I'm ready."

He attacked Africa Plate, jamming up the crack and banging in the first wedge where the plate turned left. It was a geographical trip in more ways than one. He recalled his days as Africa correspondent based in Lagos as he belted a piton in. That's one for Nigeria, now let's get across the border into Dahomey. His hammer cracked again. I'll swing past Togo and get one in at Ghana. That's where I interviewed General O'Rourke, the Mad Mercenary. Crack, that takes me to Abidjan. A couple more and I'll be round the bend at Senegal and ready to jam straight up again.

Page heard his whoop of triumph from above and got ready. She released the red rope so he could pull it up through the pitons, clipped the packs to her harness and the jumars to the white rope and braced herself on the end of the ledge, rehearsing the pendulum move in her mind.

The minute she heard his call, she screwed up her courage and threw herself into the swing, legs pumping hard, like a horizontal sprinter on a vertical track. She glimpsed the horizon tilted in front of her, as a stunt pilot would, a green wall of jungle on her left and a blue wall of sky on the right. Then the velocity of her swing overtook her and she was running to keep up with it, her feet suddenly clumsy. Stumbling, she rolled in a chaotic tangle across the rock. Her momentum carried her as far as it could until she swung back, scraping to a stop with the rope directly above. As her harness jerked her upright the world spun right way up again, sky above, jungle below.

Stunned and trembling, she somehow got her feet into the jumar loops. But as she started up she was aware she couldn't take much more. She looked up and saw Morgan leaning down to her.

"Got a surprise for you," he said.

"Another hundred-foot crack?"

"Better."

"A great ugly overhang?"

He burst into the stirring lyric of the famous Welsh rugby song, "Sospan fach . . ." Then he leaned down again.

"This is the top, my love."

She pulled up the last few feet and flung her arms around him. They laughed and slapped each other on the back and looked around the flat summit.

"Dave, we did it! We're here! What a climb!"

"How's it feel being where no one else has ever been before?"

"It's the most exciting thing I've ever done."

"Well, while you've still got that triumphant glow I want a picture of you for the story," Morgan said. " 'Foster Reaches Lost World.' "

He stopped the aperture down to f22 against the bright sunlight. Page heard the shutter click and sank down on a pack to survey the rolling green world below.

To the northwest the walls of the Carichana plateau rose. Other, lesser mountains lay to the north and east. Here and there a barely visible dark line showed where a river ran. Far below, distant curtains of rain fell from low cloud groups, each with its own rainbow and flashing lightning. But they were only isolated points of turbulence under the blue sky.

She turned to Morgan. "Have you ever seen anything like this?"

"No. Nowhere else is so stark and simple. A bowl of blue above and a floor of green below as far as you can see."

"We seem to be floating in space."

"That's because you can't see the sides of the mountain. Most mountains have sloping sides. Here it's sheer walls."

The summit was covered with tough green grass and sprinkled with bright yellow pitcher plants two feet tall.

"If you half-close your eyes it looks like spring in Wales with the daffodils running riot," he said.

Page laughed. "Well, let's go for a walk in the meadows. I want to see over the other side."

He picked up the packs. "Come on then. We've got time for a tour before we go down to the cave. We'll circle round and come back to that tree over there on the edge. That'll be our first belay."

They started off and Page stooped to examine an orange flower on a tall stem like a tulip's. "I've never seen this."

"It might be a new species," Morgan said. "I talked with some botanists and they thought that most of the plants growing up here don't grow anywhere else."

"But I've seen this before, the one with the dark green leaf. It's a *Stegolepys pulchella*. And look at this one, it's a mountain everardia."

"They're all shrubs to me, I'm afraid. C'mon, if we get over to the southwest edge we can look across to the Cerro Wichaj. It's a bad-magic mountain, according to the Piaroa Indians."

The plateau spread away from them level on all sides as they neared the center. Here and there the thin coating of earth gave way to red porous rock, rough and pitted as a petrified sponge. At the western edge big hawks—*gavilanes* and *zamurros*—shot up into view and soared away on the updraft of wind.

Morgan stopped so suddenly that Page bumped into him from behind. "What the devil is that?" he said dropping the packs and advancing with his eyes on the ground. "Come and look."

He was pointing and she saw a circular area about twenty feet across where the pitcher plants were flattened, or broken and scattered.

"That's odd," he said. "It couldn't be wind or rain because it would affect a wider area. I'll be damned. Look at this."

Page went to him. The ground had been disturbed. There was a long shallow indentation as if a heavy pole had lain there. Morgan looked up and saw a similar imprint eight feet away. Immediately he understood.

"We've been beaten. These are the marks of a helicopter. Somebody's been here before us."

Page stared at him. She almost felt like crying. "Damn. A lousy helicopter. Why didn't we come up here that way?"

Morgan shook his head in disgust. "It would have cost an arm and a leg. And besides, we would have missed that beautiful climb."

"But who could it be?" she asked.

He shrugged. "It must be a survey team. The government has geologists working this whole area. They're investigating the Guiana Shield and how these plateaus were formed."

"Do you think they got down to the cave?"

"They wouldn't have the technique."

"I hope you're right."

Her disappointment was plain and Morgan appreciated it.

"Damn," she said. "Lousy geologists. What right have they got to be up here?"

He patted her on the shoulder. "Cheer up. There's still at least one unexplored wonder in this overpopulated world of ours and we're going to be the first to see it."

In The Eye
Of The Gods

11

Morgan took a firm grip on the rope and leaned back over the edge. He glanced down two thousand feet to the jungle. Steeper than the rappel off the Grépon in the Alps.

He had put all their equipment and food in one pack. Now he adjusted it on his shoulders and looked up at Page, who was tied to the belay tree.

"You look a little pale, moppet."

"I'm scared."

"It's only four hundred feet and think of the prize at the end. We'll be the first mortals to look into the Eye of the Gods."

He rappelled down 100 feet, 120 feet, searching the rock below for a ledge. A hundred and thirty feet, 140 feet. Not a resting place in sight. The climber's nightmare, coming to the end of his rope with not even a wrinkle in the rock to stand on.

It was time to rely on a bolt. He attached jumars to the rope and clipped them to his harness so that he hung with his hands free. He took his hammer from its sheath and unclipped the steel star drill from its loop on his belt. The drill was six inches long and a quarter-inch thick, the type construction workers use to punch holes in concrete beams. Morgan preferred it to the purpose-made three-part punches in the fancy climbing shops. He had wound a couple yards of tape round the middle to give a grip. Now he held the drill against the rock and hefted his short heavy hammer.

Let's see how many fracture lines we get in this sandstone. One and we'll have to start over again.

He hit hard and the star-shaped point bit into the rock. He gave the drill a half turn and hit again. He repeated the movement, hit and twist, hit and twist. He counted to keep the rhythm up, forty and twist, forty-one and twist, forty-two. At sixty the sweat was running and his forearms were swollen hard. Damned hard rock this. Eighty-five and twist, eighty-six. He stopped and eased the drill out to measure the depth of the hole. An inch and a quarter and no fracture lines.

"That'll do," he said clipping the drill to its loop and slipping the hammer into its sheath.

He took a bolt and its ring plate from the nylon pouch on his belt and pushed it into the hole as far as he could, about half an inch. With his hammer he gave the bolt a careful tap. As it drove home he hit harder listening to the dry crack of the hammer and watching intently for fractures.

The bolt went in and Morgan tapped it with his finger. "Right, you bastard, don't flip out when I put my weight on you."

He clipped a carabiner into the ring plate, unclipped the jumars and let his weight come on the bolt. It held. And you'd better go on holding, he thought, because Page is going to be hanging here too in a minute.

Up top Page saw the rope slacken as Morgan transferred his weight to the bolt. This was the signal for her to start. She threaded the rope through her carabiner and its brake bar and stepped back over the edge. She gasped as she saw the jungle far below, then gritted her teeth and started down.

When she reached Morgan, she was given no time to squeak about both of them being suspended from one bolt. He grabbed her. "Got you," he said. "You can't take your hands off the rope or you'll drop to a dreadful death, so I'm free to fondle your gorgeous tits."

It did the trick. Page relaxed and he tickled her as he deftly clipped her to the bolt, hauled down the rope, clipped it to a second carabiner on the ring plate, kissed her and slid down on the second rappel.

"So long, luv, see you downstairs."

They made the remaining rappels without incident. Page completed the last one down to the ledge that formed the threshold of the cave and saw that it sloped steeply outward to a broken edge. She noticed a smaller ledge below. At least they'd have a landing place on their first rappel when they left the cave, even if the rest was a straight drop to the jungle.

She unclipped the rope and joined Morgan, who was standing looking into the cave.

The entrance was one hundred feet wide and rose above them in a curved arch ten stories high. Standing in it they could look straight through the mountain and out through the opening on the other side, three hundred feet away. It formed a pointed arch like a huge church window and framed a patch of sky.

Light streamed through both openings and glowed on the red, yellow and white walls. Halfway along the right wall was a large dark tunnel. Beyond it, near the other side, was an arched opening that seemed to lead to a second chamber. Along the left wall were several smaller tunnels.

The roof was of red rock. It ran level and then rose in the center at a ninety degree angle to form a dome rounded out in a geometric half sphere fifteen stories high.

The floor was the size of a football field and had the same rectangular shape. Except for the odd pile of jagged blocks fallen from the roof it was almost as flat as a city plaza.

With its domed roof the chamber was as big as a cathedral. It was like St. Paul's stuck up inside a mountain. Eye of the Gods, Morgan thought. That's what it looks like from below. Up here it's more like the Hall of the Gods.

"I can't believe it," Page said.

"Nobody will unless we take some pictures. Why don't you get your photo gear out and I'll haul the rope down. Get the flashlights while you're at it."

She put five rolls of color film and four of fast, 400 ASA black-and-white in her photo bag, and a small telephoto and 28mm wide-angle lens. She stopped her camera down to f8 and shutter speed 125.

"I need a picture of you standing in the entrance," Morgan said. "Intrepid explorer entering Cuyakiare's den."

"Okay, I'll stand over here holding the rope."

He took two shots and handed her the camera. "By the way have you ever stopped to think what you'd do if there really was a dinosaur up here?"

"I'm sure I could rely on you."

"You could rely on me to take a running dive off the mountain."

"Well before you jump I want a shot of you over there with the jungle below."

"Right. How's this?"

He stood on the edge, raised his arms in terror and leaned back.

"David! Don't do that!"

"Did you get the shot?"

"No, I didn't. You scared the life out of me. Stop clowning and let me take a picture."

She took the picture. "Are we ready to go?" he said.

"Ready."

"Okay, how are we going to go about this?"

"What d'you mean?"

"I mean what are you going to do now that you're up here?"

"I'm going to explore and take pictures."

Morgan took out his silver-fob watch and flipped open the lid. Page grinned at this battered, unshaven tramp holding his old-fashioned timepiece in his grimy hand with his cuts and bruises and cracked fingernails.

"You didn't forget your gold monocle, did you?"

"My what?"

"Nothing. What time is it?"

"It's eleven-thirty. We can look around for an hour and then have something to eat. Then we'll poke about some more and by that time it'll be dark. You want to spend the night, I take it."

"Of course, think how romantic it'll be."

"Aren't you afraid you'll be eaten alive? I thought you believed in dinosaurs."

"If I did it's because I read your book."

"There you go again, blaming my book." He glanced around the cave. "So all right, we'll spend the night and then rappel down in the morning. We don't have all that much food, you know."

"Tomorrow morning! I thought we were going to stay a few days. I didn't climb all the way up here just to eat and run."

"I'm sort of anxious to get back to Caracas," Morgan said.

"You're tired of me already?"

"You know it's not that. I'm worried about Mabruk and the King."

"Morgan the vulturous newsman."

"Okay, okay. Let's see how it works out. Are we ready?"

"Let's go."

They walked in. The floor was covered with small white stones. Page picked one up.

"You can see the action of water here. Look how these stones are worn flat and smooth. It's like a riverbed."

"You may be right," Morgan said. "I showed a photo of the mountain to a geologist and he thought the cave might have been formed by water."

"He's right. There's a new theory about it. I saw a paper on it by a man named Pablo Colvet."

"I wish I'd known about it when I wrote the book. I had to leave it as another riddle of the mysterious Autana."

"Among many," Page said dryly.

"Spare me the cracks," Morgan laughed, "and tell me the theory."

"Over millions of years rain found its way down fissures in the mountain and hollowed out tunnels like those over there."

"What about the dome?"

"The tunnels got blocked by roof falls and the water formed whirlpools, sweeping big boulders around the walls. They ground out the dome."

"Very neat. That would account for how round and smooth it is."

They were directly under the dome's apex now. On the left was a pile of fallen blocks. Page motioned with her camera.

"I'd like a picture of you on top of those rocks with the dome above. I can get it with the wide-angle lens."

"Anything to oblige."

Morgan climbed onto the pile and stood looking up heroically at the wall. Page took a picture and cocked her head composing another shot.

She walked twenty yards toward the other entrance and stopped to gauge the range. She rummaged in her bag.

"Hold it while I put the telephoto lens on."

She focused on Morgan. When the blurred image became clear, she saw he was looking down this time. What's got into him, she thought; he's behaving like a perfect model, standing still like that. She clicked the shutter, opened up one stop and focused again. What happened to the clowning? He's like a statue for heaven's sake, Hamlet at the graveside. She clicked again.

"Okay, it's done."

Morgan didn't move. He was still staring at his feet.

Page shrugged, changed lenses and turned away to explore. She had no plan, only her enthusiasm to guide her. This resulted in a series of false starts. Looking across to the other opening she noted a rectangular block of rock that had fallen in the entrance. A person standing on it would look as small as if he were on the prow of a schooner. Bet the view from it is terrific, she thought. Probably can see all the way to Brazil.

She started toward it but paused before the large tunnel on her right. It was dark. She dug her flashlight out and flicked a beam into it. This was no more effective than a car headlight in thick fog. She swept the beam around the ceiling and walls and took a step forward. She went a little farther, keeping the light on the floor to see where she was going. The ground was level and unobstructed but each step was harder for her to take than the last. The darkness was discouraging. Finally she came to a halt about twenty feet inside, reluctant to proceed. She stood listening. Silence. If the Autana was really honeycombed with tunnels from top to bottom as the Indians believed, this one might go all the way down through the mountain. She drew a breath to see how far a shout would carry before it came back to her, but changed her mind. Instead, meekly she said, "Is anyone home?"

Her voice sounded very flat and lonely. She felt foolish. What're you beginning to believe in, ghosts . . . or dinosaurs? But she wanted no more of it. I want company when I explore this one.

On her way out she tried to maintain a dignified pace, but her real impulse carried her straight across the cave in the opposite direction toward the series of smaller tunnels in the other wall. Somehow they seemed less forbidding. She barely looked at Morgan, who was still standing on the pile of rubble as if he had been turned to stone.

"Come on," she called over her shoulder.

She reached the tunnels and walked a few yards into one, marveling at the nearly perfect curve of the walls. This was another false start. At a bend the tunnel receded into darkness. Company here too, she thought. As she turned to go she noticed a tiny white object on a ledge near the ceiling. It was a minute skull in a cluster of delicate bones.

A bird? She picked up the skull and examined it. It was like no bird she could recall. The skull was too short, almost flat-faced. Must have been an ugly, pug-faced creature. Of course! A bat. She peered closer in the half light. There were dozens of tiny skeletons. Extraordinary, she thought, a bat cemetery. Must tell David about it.

She cradled the skull in her hand to take it across the cave to Morgan. But as she started out of the tunnel he was there, right in front of her.

He grabbed her and his voice was urgent. "We're getting out of here."

"What d'you mean? We just got here."

"Come on, dammit, do as I say."

She twisted her arm free. "What are you whispering about? You're not making any sense."

How do you get it over to people, Morgan thought. It had happened to him before. He was taking a risky shortcut across a lonely moor in Wales and there was this woman standing there admiring the view. He stopped his motorbike next to her car. "Lady," he said, "this is an army firing range. We have to get out of here." "What?" she said. "You're talking nonsense, it's so peaceful."

"Look, Page," he said holding out his hand. "See this?"

Page looked. "It's a ballpoint pen. So what?"

"See this emblem? It's the national symbol of El Hajjaz."

"El Hajjaz?" His alarm had begun to get to her. "I don't understand."

He was facing the woman on the moor. "Lady, you see this thing here? It's a shell case." The woman frowned at him. "I don't understand," she said.

"Page, Mabruk hands these pens out to newsmen as a public relations gimmick. I just found this on those rocks. Let's go for crissake."

Page wouldn't budge. "C'mon, Morgan, you're trying to scare me. You had that pen when you came to my hotel. You lent it to me to write down directions."

The woman on the moor looked at the shell case. "You could've had that for years," she said. He rounded on her. "Why you pig-headed old frump, I just picked it up. I don't know why I'm standing here arguing with you. I should kick you into your car and chase you the hell out of here. They're going to open fire any minute. We're going to get a shell up our asses . . ."

"Foster, you stubborn twit, that was my own pen. Look," he reached for his shirt pocket, "I've got two of them. One of these Mabruk gave me at the airport when he arrived in Venezuela. The other I just picked up this minute."

He stood before her holding up the two ballpoint pens, one in each hand, identical. One moment Page was looking at them anxiously, still not sure if he was joking. The next, her head jerked up.

Morgan glanced behind him, following her gaze. He was back on the firing range. He saw two men coming along the passageway from the second chamber. They were both carrying submachine guns.

12

"Don't move!" the bigger of the two men shouted. "Get your hands up!"

Morgan's hands went up, still holding the ballpoint pens. He felt like a fool standing there holding up two ballpoint pens at shoulder level. But he didn't feel foolish enough to lower his hands or even to drop the pens. He suspected that's all it would take to get them both shot.

"David!" Page gasped. Her own hands went up.

"Just do as they say," he told her.

The two men approached with their machine guns. "Don't try anything!" the bigger shouted.

They were both in street clothes. One was a squat little fireplug of a man, half Indian. The other was over six feet and on the flabby side, not exactly fat but getting there . . . And then, as the two came up, Morgan saw the bigger one's face and he had that shock of recognition you get when you're drinking at your favorite pub and all of a sudden you look up and the man standing next to you at the bar is a famous movie star.

The difference was that the last time Morgan had seen the face it was on a wanted poster pasted to a kiosk in Frankfurt, Germany. The man was known as the most wanted man in the world. A fair description. Currently twelve countries were after him.

Morgan's brain did a biographical printout. Leon Trotsky Suárez, alias Emiliano, alias the Wolf. Born in Venezuela twenty-six years ago. Son of a Marxist university professor, who had named him after the Russian revolutionary. Attended Patrice Lumumba University in Moscow. Learned weaponry, sabotage and killer karate at institutes run by the KGB. Trained in terrorism during a summer with the Popular Front for the Liberation of Palestine in Jordan.

Morgan had once interviewed his father. The old man had gone on about how politically he was in complete agreement with his son although they might diverge a bit on strategic matters. Meanwhile the son was off shooting people, hijacking planes and smuggling arms: "strategic matters."

He had last been reported to be in Yugoslavia, which had ignored requests by Austria, France and the United States to detain him before putting him on a plane to Baghdad. Now nobody knew for sure where he was.

Except he's home, Morgan thought. And who would ever guess he was behind Mabruk's kidnapping.

It didn't make sense. Why would a man like Emiliano risk his neck to get an amateur like Jules Smith out of jail? But there was no other explanation. Emiliano had been the leader of the men in the surgical masks. They had grabbed Karim and brought him to the Autana. That explained the helicopter tracks up top. Somewhere in the caves Karim was being held prisoner.

Morgan and Page stood with their hands up and there was a rapid exchange in Spanish between Emiliano and the short one.

"Chucho," Emiliano barked, "did you see any others?"

"No, commandante!"

"Where did they come from?"

"Over by the entrance."

"Hurry and take a look!"

The short one named Chucho darted away. Tough little monkey, good at taking orders. Probably recruited from one of the shantytowns around Caracas.

Emiliano turned, shaking his gun at Morgan. He spoke in English now. "Who are you! What are you doing here!"

"We're nobody," Morgan said. "We were just mountain climbing."

"Is anybody with you?"

"No, we're alone."

"Don't lie, you motherfucker, or I'll blow your head off!"

Marvelous command of the idiom, Morgan thought, remembering how proud the old man had been of his son's ability with languages. Spoke six fluently: Spanish, German, French, English, Russian and Arabic. Of course he got around quite a bit.

"Who knows you're here?" Emiliano said.

Morgan considered bluffing: the whole Venezuelan Army is coming down from up top. But he knew it would backfire as soon as Emiliano found out he was lying.

"Four Indians," he said. "They brought us upriver. They're waiting for us below."

"Who else?"

"No one that can hurt you."

Emiliano shook his gun threateningly. "Who!"

He was trembling, which was surprising, Morgan thought, since he was alleged to be a very cool customer. He didn't expect us to drop in like this. Can't blame him. Who would ever expect company all the way up here? You go out of your way to find a safe hiding place and all of a sudden two strangers show up. Well he's not trembling any more than I am. Morgan's hands were shaking as if the pens were two high-tension wires.

"I'm telling you," he said, "we're just on a climb. Nobody really knows we're up here except those Indians."

The answer seemed to satisfy Emiliano. He glanced toward the main opening where the short one was, the interrogation over.

Morgan studied his face. For all his aliases it was an old boyhood nickname that fit him best, at least physically. El Gordo, the Fat One. The face chubby with thick, sensual lips and heavy-lidded eyes, the face of a spoiled mama's boy.

"What's happening," Page said. "Who are they?"

The face jerked around. "Shut up."

"Don't worry," Morgan told her. "Do as he says."

He was afraid, but he was sure they would get out of this alive if they didn't try anything. They would be kept prisoners along with Karim and all three of them would be released, he hoped, when Jules Smith was. Emiliano wouldn't want to jeopardize his credibility as a negotiator. Otherwise no one would deal with him next time. When word got out that he was behind the kidnapping, his reputation as a man of his word would be secure.

Chucho came back, the stones clacking beneath his feet. "*Nada.* A rope, some climbing stuff. Nobody else."

Emiliano stepped up, holding the muzzle of his machine gun under Morgan's chin. It was a Magdanich D-12. Hollow stock, capable of firing 360 slugs a minute. He frisked him roughly, punching him in the balls. Something you always appreciated. He took the flashlight from his pocket and grabbed Page's, leaving the camera around her neck. Then he motioned at them with his gun.

"All right, let's go."

Morgan was shoved into the passageway where the gunmen had come from. It was lower and narrower than the main cave and at the end, as he had guessed, it opened up into a second chamber. They were marched along the passageway and he cursed their luck.

Why, out of all the hideouts in the world, had the kidnappers chosen the Autana? It was an unacceptable coincidence. On reflection, though, it was all too acceptable. The authorities would be combing every city and town and have roadblocks on all the roads. In the time it took for the ransom demand to be met the dragnet would tighten. But no dragnet would ever reach out here, Morgan knew.

That's how they had been able to get away so effectively. It was one thing to kidnap a man from his home and another to do it in public and still manage to escape.

He saw how it must have been done. Emiliano had known about the Autana. Before the kidnapping he had flown out to check the landing site and lay in supplies. After the kidnapping he had ditched the ambulance and transferred to another car. The helicopter had been waiting someplace nearby. They had been in the air and out over the jungle before the authorities knew what hit them. A few hours later they had set down on the Autana. Karim wasn't a climber. They must have lowered him to the cave entrance from the helicopter and they would haul him back up when it was time to go. There wasn't much he could say about it. These fellows weren't noted for their deference to royalty.

Morgan was wondering how Karim had stood up under it all when, just then, as they approached an alcove that branched off from the large chamber they were entering, there he was, sitting on the ground with his back against a rock, reading a paperback book by the light from one of the smaller openings in the mountain.

The alcove wasn't the worst jail Morgan had ever seen. It had a rustic charm. There was a slender tree with delicate leafy branches growing in the center, and a spring welled up among the white stones, trickling out into the chamber before going underground again. Plenty of light and air. Nice view. Even a radio on the rock Karim was sitting against. Morgan had spent the night in worse hotel rooms.

Karim was wearing the same charcoal-gray London-tailored suit, ripped halfway up the back, that he had been kidnapped in. Morgan's first thought was, Poor bastard, to be in the hands of these shits.

He hoped they would all be free before long. That's what the radio was for: to listen for the announcement of Smith's release. Morgan had no doubt the ransom demand would be met. The King wouldn't play games with his nephew's life. Maybe, for all he knew, it had already happened: Smith had been flown to Libya and now Emiliano was waiting for the helicopter to pick them up. Instead of one prisoner he would have three. If the three were lucky they would be left tied up at the side of some road, covered with bruises and cigarette burns but alive, which was the usual procedure. From the way Karim looked, it couldn't happen too soon. He looked worried.

Well, you would too, Morgan thought, if you had been yanked from the steps of the Central Bank into an ambulance by a gang of thugs who couldn't wait to work you over as a form of political indoctrination. Nothing you liked to see happen to an old friend . . . but wait a minute, wait a minute . . .

The instant Karim saw him he jumped up with a look of shock, dropping his book.

"David! My God what are *you* doing here!"

"Mabruk! Are you all right!"

Morgan was thinking, Wait a minute, wait a minute, suddenly so confused that he forgot how ridiculous he felt holding up the two pens. Wait a minute . . .

Because Karim wasn't looking at him anymore. He was gaping at Emiliano and there was another rapid exchange, this time in English.

"Suárez, what's wrong!"

"They were wandering around out there."

"But I thought you said we were safe!"

"We are safe. There's nobody but these two."

Karim was wild. He was pacing back and forth, completely ignoring Morgan. It was hardly what you would expect from an old friend.

"Do you know who this man is!" he cried. "He's a friend of the King's!"

"The King!" Emiliano exclaimed.

"I knew something was wrong when the announcement didn't come! They must know where we are! This is all your fault! You said we were safe!"

"But how could they find out?" Emiliano protested. "If they knew where we were they'd have the whole army down here, not these two. They're just mountain climbing. The only people who know they're up here are some Indians." He grabbed Morgan by the collar, jamming the Magdanich into his face. "Isn't that right, you stinking shit! Unless you were lying!"

Abruptly Karim ceased pacing and stooped to pick up the book he had dropped. When he straightened up it was to face Morgan with a look of dawning surprise and relief.

"Mountain climbing! Of course! You mentioned your trip the other day."

And now Morgan was saying what he had only been thinking before, "Wait a minute, wait a minute . . ."

Karim cocked his head toward him. He was Morgan's friend again.

"You mean you're not a prisoner?" Morgan said.

Karim threw up his arms in a gesture that contained a little bit of everything: amazement, chagrin, irony, regret.

"Of course I'm not a prisoner! You gave me a hell of a fright!"

13

Now Morgan knew that the news was truly his curse. Even when he wasn't chasing it, it followed him around. It was like some sort of beast, a shaggy dog, say, that you trained to obey you so that after a while it wasn't you that depended on it to earn a living, it was the news that depended on you to keep it going, feed it, a big lumbering animal that never left you alone.

So he figured maybe they're trying to tell him something. You go after a story that you know doesn't exist and what do you end up with? The same old news. Maybe all you'll have to do from now on, providing you get out of this alive, which is beginning to look doubtful, is to sit home and wait for the news to come to you instead of the other way around. There's a knock at the door and you go to it and it's an earthquake. So you invite the earthquake in and sit down and have a chat with it. Hello, how are you? Been quaking lately? Jolly good. Well, cheerio. Nice of you to drop by. And then you phone it in to Gordon, who got you into this in the first place so he could appease the great god Circulation. Or maybe it's a flood. Or an election campaign, the whole lot of them, the candidates and the voters, trooping into your living room and drinking your whiskey and sleeping with your girl friend. Or maybe a kidnap victim. That would be good. Especially if the victim turned out not to be a victim. Turned out to be the kidnapper. Think of how simple it would be if all the kidnappers in the world began to kidnap themselves. First kidnapper: "Pulled off any good jobs lately?" Second kidnapper: "Oh yes. Spent the weekend in the trunk of my car. Worth every penny I had to pay myself to get out."

Only Karim would have himself kidnapped in full view, right on those beautiful fifteen steps of the Central in downtown Caracas, and a bloody good show it was, too, very convincing they were about it, even had real corpses, hauled him off in an ambulance that looked just like the real thing and shortly afterward comes this phone call demanding the release of a nice fellow who goes around blowing young girls' heads off and the next time you see Karim he's in the company of a regular celebrity, a person who's right up there with Jack the Ripper . . . why would he go through all that trouble . . . unless, of course, he was a friend of the nice fellow's.

"So you're with *them*," Morgan said.

But Karim was ignoring him again, eager to explain everything to Emiliano.

"Can you believe it! I know this man! He said he was going on an expedition! But I never dreamed it would be here!"

"I told you," Emiliano said, letting go of Morgan's collar with a shove. He was angry at having been accused.

"But how was I to know! The minute I saw him I was sure we had been found out."

Page was confused. But she wasn't less afraid now, because the man standing before them seemed to be Morgan's friend.

"Who is he? she asked.

"It's Prince Karim," he told her.

"I thought he was kidnapped," she said.

"So does everyone else."

Karim laughed. "You should never trust appearances, David. You know that."

Morgan remembered the picture of Jules Smith that had been in all the papers after he surrendered. He was being taken away by two plainclothesmen who each had a look of horror on his face, no doubt from the mess they had just seen in the room of the Holiday Inn. The young American between them, on the other hand, wearing a white linen suit and with his wrists handcuffed before him, was smiling as if he knew something the two horrified plainclothesmen didn't. Now Morgan understood. It was the smile of someone who had a friend in high places.

"Why would you want to get a bloodthirsty bastard like Jules Smith out of jail?" he said sourly. "How long have you been in with these fellows?"

Karim shook his head. "David, David, always asking questions."

"It's not every day I get shoved around like this."

"I'm sorry. If you had only told me you were coming up here we would have changed our plans."

I'll bet, Morgan thought. He said, "That was quite a show you put on in front of the bank. Scared the hell out of me."

"It scared me," Karim said, "and I knew it was going to happen."

"You had me fooled."

That's right, Morgan thought, stick to small talk. Instead of asking him what's really on your mind. He had asked a lot of questions in his life and this was the first time he had ever been afraid of getting an answer. Small talk was much better. And this was a pleasant place for it with its tree and bubbling brook and the sunlight and fresh air coming in through the opening. It was like being on a picnic. Except who would ever go on a picnic in a custom-tailored suit with the jacket ripped halfway up the back?

"They did a job on your suit," he said.

"Yes, that was carrying realism a bit far. And the worst thing was they forgot to bring along a change of clothes. And I don't know how much longer I'm going to have to be up here."

"It's quite a ways to go to hole up."

"Ah well, Suárez felt the cities were too risky. So we came here. Would you believe, they lowered me from a helicopter."

"I don't think you'll have to stay much longer. Hasn't Smith been released yet?"

Karim flung up his arms. "No! That's just it! He hasn't!" He had the look of someone who has just been reminded that he's suffering from a fatal disease. "The announcement's long overdue. I've been listening to the radio every hour."

"Sometimes these things take time."

"I hope you're right." Karim glanced at his wristwatch as if to see how much time he had left.

"It seems like an awful lot of trouble just to get somebody out of jail," Morgan said. "Is he a friend of yours?"

"Not really. I'm afraid there's more to it than that."

Wait a minute, wait a minute, Morgan thought. More? "What more?"

Karim didn't wish to say. "I trust you got a good story out of the kidnapping," he said. "Remember, I suggested you be there."

"For a moment I thought I was going to get shot."

"You needn't have worried. I told Suárez to be sure not to shoot any newsmen."

"I hope you still mean it," Morgan said impulsively.

The words were out before he knew it. He was almost as startled as Karim evidently was, by the look on his face. So it was no use stalling any longer, he thought. Might as well ask him and get it over with.

"*Do* you mean it?" he said.

Karim avoided his eyes. "I really don't know what to do. You've put me in a terrible position. I don't know who this woman is . . ."

"What does that have to do with it?" Morgan was getting the answer he had feared.

Karim faced him helplessly. "Why did you have to come up here? How can I let you go? If there was some way I could trust you . . ."

"Trust him!" Emiliano broke in. "You can't trust him! We've got to shoot them!"

"Yes, yes," Karim said impatiently and turned away as if he didn't wish to discuss it any further, slipping the paperback book into his jacket pocket.

"But why?" Morgan said. "I don't care who you hang out with or what your politics are."

"You've caught me up here, David. That's enough."

"But this woman doesn't even know you."

Page couldn't believe what Karim was saying. "I thought you were David's friend!" she said.

Karim faced her, opening his arms. It was the first time he had really bothered to look at her.

"I am his friend," he said. "Do you think I want to do this? I haven't any choice."

She turned to Morgan for support but he couldn't give it to her. Karim had had himself kidnapped and was in with the terrorists. He couldn't afford to let that get out. If the King ever found out he'd be finished.

"I'm sorry," Morgan told her. "I should have got you out of here the minute I found his pen."

Karim raised his eyebrows, patting his breast pocket with one hand and indicating one of the ballpoint pens with his other as if he had just noticed Morgan was holding them.

"I knew I must have dropped it somewhere," he said.

"You can have them," Morgan said. "You might need them to write your memoirs."

Karim's face darkened. "Well, if you don't mind . . ." Without looking at Morgan he removed the two pens and slipped them into his pocket. "I'm always losing things. I'd probably lose my head if it wasn't attached to my neck."

"You might lose it anyway when the King finds out."

Karim's head jerked up as if from an insult. "He won't find out."

"I wouldn't be so sure. He's a shrewd man. You can't fool him forever."

"I won't have to fool him forever," Karim said.

"What do you mean?"

"I'm afraid the King's not long for this world."

"What are you up to, Mabruk?" Morgan demanded.

Karim turned away with that same impatience as before.

"Is it something you're ashamed of?"

No answer.

"Why be ashamed. Apparently we are not going to be around to tell anybody. What are you up to?"

No answer.

Morgan kept after him. "I thought you didn't like guns. You always told me you disapproved of your uncle's hunting. I guess hunting's all right as long as it's people who are getting shot. Is that it?" He saw Karim's back stiffen. "First it's that girl in El Hajjaz. Then it's those people on the steps of the bank. And now it's us. Who else have you got in mind, you murderous bastard?"

Karim whirled. His face was purple.

"You know, David, you should have been a lawyer after all. You could make the hardest case confess."

"What are you up to?" Morgan said hoarsely. "What are you up to?"

"I'm surprised you haven't guessed," Karim said. "We're going to assassinate the King."

14

Karim stood before them in his rumpled suit in this incongruous setting, the alcove a cool refuge from the heat and glare of the jungle below, and he was the same man Morgan had known since Cambridge. But now Morgan was beginning to wonder if he had ever really known him.

Funny, he thought, how having a gun stuck in your back can turn old friends into strangers.

He didn't understand what having yourself kidnapped or getting Jules Smith out of jail had to do with assassinating the King. But he was too scared to figure it out. Page was standing beside him with her hands up, looking as if she still couldn't believe what was happening while Chucho, the short one, stood behind her with his gun at her back. She looks about the way I feel, Morgan thought.

He knew he had to do something. He could grab for Emiliano's gun and that would be an end to it right there. Or he and Page could make a break for it. But where could they go, even if they weren't cut down immediately? They were stuck up inside a mountain. Joaquín was below and there was nothing he could do to help them. The only thing Morgan could think of was to play for time. So he had to be polite.

"Why would you want to kill the King?" he said.

Karim scowled. He didn't like being called a murderous bastard. "Some things are necessary for the good of the people."

"The people love him.

Morgan felt as if he were performing a parody of civilization, as if the essence of civilization was an ability to carry on a conversation in the face of death.

"They love him because he's backward like themselves" Karim said. "An old fool who sleeps in a goatskin tent. A pawn to Western imperialism."

"He was never a pawn to anybody."

Karim shrugged. He didn't wish to argue.

"For someone you despise so much," Morgan said, "he's doing a lot of worrying about your skin."

"I'm beginning to wonder," Karim said bitterly. He was silent a moment. He faced Morgan as if to lecture him.

"We've been up here since Thursday afternoon. At first we heard that the King was issuing no statement. Then he announced that the ransom demand would be met. On Friday he resumed the loan talks, which we expected. As a matter of fact we were counting on it."

"Counting on it?" Morgan said.

Karim ignored the question. "On the same day he asked the council of citizens to release Jules Smith. A mere formality . . . or so we thought. Instead they chose to debate the matter all Saturday. I think I know which parties are to blame for this. Nevertheless, we certainly expected the announcement by this morning."

"You know your uncle can overrule the council."

"Then why in God's name hasn't he . . . after all the trouble we've gone through to provide him with a ransom demand that he could meet?"

"I'll wager he has, if he's been com—" Morgan stopped. He saw it now, or at least part of it. "I see. You don't care about Smith. He's just your ransom demand."

"Of course." Karim waved his hand as if the fact were obvious. "It's easy to have yourself kidnapped, David. I'm beginning to realize it's not so easy to be released. I can't very well turn up alive unless the demand is met. It wouldn't look right."

So that was it, Morgan thought. It was all for the sake of appearances. If you were going to have yourself kidnapped you had to arrange for a release that "looked right." Otherwise people would suspect something. So they had given the King a ransom demand in his own country that he could meet without too much trouble. The irony was that they couldn't assassinate him until he had "saved" Karim.

"Did killing that girl in El Hajjaz look right?" Morgan said. He was finding it harder to be civilized.

"I had nothing to do with that," Karim said. "It was Suárez who hired Smith."

"You wanted him to get arrested for a terrorist act," Emiliano spoke up, defending himself.

Karim gave him a sour look over Morgan's shoulder. "He didn't have to kill the girl."

"That was up to him."

Morgan saw how tension had been building between the two men in the last three days. Karim had engaged Emiliano to do a job for him and the job seemed to be going wrong.

"I just hope he hasn't talked," Karim said.

"I told you he doesn't know anything," Emiliano said. "Do you think I would have told him who was paying us and for what?"

"Then why hasn't he been released? Do you realize that if this drags on until the loan talks are finished we'll have lost our chance?"

"Stop worrying. He'll be released. Listen to the radio. You've probably missed it."

Karim glanced at his wristwatch again. Emiliano gave an order to Chucho in Spanish.

Chucho skipped across the spring to where the radio sat. Watching him Morgan thought he resembled a monkey who had been trained to turn on a radio.

There was a crackle of static within which rose the voice of Pedro Blanco singing *"No llores, mi amor, yo nunca te olvidaré."* That was reassuring, Morgan thought. But he felt cold inside and his raised arms were getting tired and he didn't know how much longer Emiliano could be kept from shooting them. In the meantime all

Pedro Blanco could offer was "Don't cry, my love, I'll never forget you."

Morgan still couldn't see what having yourself kidnapped had to do with assassinating the King, unless . . . he tried to put it together and suddenly the pieces fit . . . unless it was a way of giving Karim a good excuse not to be where something terrible was going to happen . . .

In the same instant he realized why Karim had been counting on the resumption of the loan talks.

Just then Pedro Blanco ceased never forgetting and the news came on. The newscaster sounded like he was about to burst a blood vessel. The first item was the one Karim had been waiting for.

"El Rey de El Hajjaz anuncío hoy . . ."

Morgan translated for Page. "They're releasing Smith and flying him to Libya this afternoon."

Karim looked up with relief.

"What did I tell you," Emiliano said.

"You were right. I should have been more patient."

Chucho turned off the radio, cutting the newscaster's apoplectic voice off in mid-sentence, and Emiliano jabbed Morgan in the kidney with his gun.

"Let's get rid of these two," he said to Karim. "I'll take them to the other side so you won't have to shed any tears."

Chucho had started on his way back across the spring. Without warning Page sprang, seizing his gun and trying to twist it from his hands.

"David, run!"

Chucho jerked away and grabbed her and Morgan's hand went out, grasping Karim by the shirt.

He was swinging him around to use as a shield, with the idea of wrestling him to the opening in the mountain and threatening to throw him out, when something struck him on the side of the head. The next thing he knew the muzzle of Emiliano's gun was screwed against his face and Karim had pulled away.

Here goes, Morgan thought. This is the end.

But Emiliano didn't fire. Instead he jerked him roughly.

"Get your hands up!"

Morgan put his hands up. He saw that Chucho had subdued Page and was covering her with his gun. Karim had stepped back with a look of surprise. Morgan was breathing hard. Politeness was impossible now.

"Doesn't it strike you as contemptible to be plotting the murder of a man who's just saved your life?"

"My uncle is very image conscious," Karim said. "If he didn't try to save my life, what would the world think of him?"

"You've got a bloody nerve."

Chucho had dragged Page back and was hanging onto her in case she got any other ideas.

"It's going to be a bomb, isn't it?" Morgan said. "That's why you had to be kidnapped. To give yourself a reason not to be at the loan talks with the King when it goes off."

For a moment Karim didn't answer. He was examining a rip in his shirt. By the time he got out of there, Morgan thought, he would look like a scarecrow.

Finally he spoke. "I wouldn't want to be sitting with the King tomorrow morning at the negotiating table."

"You bastard."

Karim was inured to insults now. He had the superior air of a man who knew he was going to go on living.

"I know what I've got to do," he said, "and I've never allowed myself the luxury of fooling myself."

"Is that your excuse?"

"I don't need an excuse." Karim fingered the rip in his shirt. "If a man doesn't get what he wants he has only himself to blame, David. I've never left anything to chance. Of course I've always pretended not to care. Admit it, when we were at Cambridge together you thought I wasn't quite serious about life. But did you really think that I would go on being just another royal hanger-on, depending on my uncle and his son to pay my gambling debts?"

Morgan stared at him. He had the feeling he had not yet heard the worst.

"Of course, they thought I was a bit of a fool too. They were busy proving their manhood by riding wild mules. But now my cousin is dead and my uncle will soon be dead too, and in neither case," he looked at Morgan with pointed contempt, "has anything been left to chance."

"You killed your cousin," Morgan said. "You killed the King's son."

From habit he remembered it as a headline: EL HAJJAZ PRINCE DIES IN PLANE CRASH. It was one of the first *Globe* headlines he had read after going to work there. He remembered the smell of the newsroom and the way the light had come in through the windows in the late afternoon, illuminating shafts of swirling dust motes.

"I did what I had to," Karim said.

His voice sounded far away to Morgan.

"And you have to kill the King."

Karim spread his palms. "You know, I really didn't think it would be necessary. The King is an old man. But his wife died a year ago and there's always the chance he might remarry. I would hate to think what sort of incentive it might be for my enemies if he had another son."

"They've quadrupled the guard around the bank since you were kidnapped," Morgan said. "No one will ever get near that negotiating table with a bomb."

"No one that isn't allowed at it already," Karim said.

Morgan couldn't help recalling their law-student days. Karim leaned toward him as if to relate the latest collegiate prank.

"Actually, David, it's very ironic. If anyone could appreciate it, you could, because you were once a victim of my uncle's mule-riding dare. Well," his face came close and he spoke the words as if he were telling a dirty joke, *"these* mules are going to be too much for the King."

When Morgan had been a cub reporter for another paper before joining the *Globe,* he had been fired for some petty infraction. The news editor and he had never gotten along. Morgan didn't think much of him either as a man or as a judge of news, and when he was fired he couldn't resist saying so even though he knew it meant he would never be able to get a decent reference from him.

Now it wasn't a reference he was losing but he felt the same urge.

He could see Karim was eager to let him in on his joke, but he wouldn't give him the satisfaction.

"You can take your mules and shove them up your treacherous yellow ass," he said.

15

Emiliano had told Karim he was taking them to the other side to shoot them so that Karim wouldn't shed any tears. Sarcastic bastard, Morgan thought. But he was grateful for the walk.

If they could get into one of the tunnels that branched off from the main cave they might escape. But it was necessary to wait. If they broke for it now, in this narrow passageway, they would certainly be cut down before they reached the other end.

They were approaching the main cave with their hands up, walking side by side with the two gunmen behind them. Page said, "I'm sorry."

Morgan looked at her. "Good God, why?"

"It's my fault for getting us into this with my silly dinosaur hunt."

"I wouldn't have missed it for the world. How were we to know these fellows would be up here?"

He wanted to tell her he was going to try to do something but that he had to wait for the right moment. But of course he couldn't tell her. He could only hope she would be ready when the right moment came. She had grabbed Chucho's gun out of desperation and had almost got them both killed. This was no time for desperation.

He gave her as significant a look as he dared and said, "Who knows, there might be a dinosaur up here after all . . . in one of the tunnels."

"Shut up and keep moving," Emiliano said.

They entered the main cave: the beautiful natural cathedral with its roseate dome, high enough to contain a fifteen-story building beneath it, and its carpet of white stones and the light streaming in through the twin openings. Morgan began searching for the likeliest tunnel. There was the series of small ones in the far wall toward which they were being marched, but these had the unpromising look of dead-end streets.

Crossing the cave, passing the large opening that was opposite the one where their climbing equipment was, picking his way over the occasional irregularities in the ground, he felt more than ever the need to play for time.

"Suárez," he said over his shoulder, "I once interviewed your father."

There was a silence. Then Emiliano said, "When?"

"A year or so ago. For the London *Globe.*"

"Oh yes, I remember the story. Somebody sent me a clipping."

Morgan recalled that Emiliano liked to hand out autographs to hostages. He wondered if he kept a scrapbook of all the stories written about him.

So go ahead, ask him a question, he thought. That's your trade, isn't it? But for the life of him he couldn't think of any questions. All he could think of was that he had to do something, grab Page and make a run for it. His mind was a blank and he felt like the greenest cub reporter on the most insignificant newspaper in the world. Think, dammit!

"I imagine Karim's paying you handsomely for your services," he said.

"Enough," Emiliano said shortly.

"He's not the easiest person to work for, I gather."

"He has his peculiarities."

This is too gossipy for the *Globe,* Morgan thought. Maybe we can get it in the *National Enquirer.*

But he was warming to the interview now and having no trouble thinking of questions. He was about to ask who was going to bring the bomb to the negotiating table, the person who would apparently be allowed in, and what it had to do with Karim's joke about mules, when just then Emiliano shoved him over against the wall and he completely forgot the question and his mind was a blank again.

They had reached the other side of the main cave and he and Page were standing together with their backs to the wall, and Emiliano and Chucho had stepped back from them and now time was running very fast.

Say something, Morgan thought. Anything, no matter how lame. You were allowed to sound lame if you were about to be shot. Any old excuse to delay. Mind if I tie my shoe? Take a leak? Have a cigarette? That was the traditional one, wasn't it? The last cigarette before the firing squad? Funny how a silly habit could establish itself like that. Sticking this thing in your mouth and puffing away. Some primitive oral gratification. Bad for you. And yet people did it. Or they tried to give it up, as Page said she had: turning thirty and deciding to quit smoking, as if it was hard enough for her to face the fact of mortality without adding to it the insult of this simple, senseless human craving. But there it was, an accepted tradition, the last cigarette, and while Morgan had never been one to stand on tradition, he felt in this case there was something to be said for it.

"Mind if I have a cigarette?" he said.

He had always prided himself on his ability to deliver bad news. That's what reporting was all about. You didn't waste your time with good news. It was only the bad that counted. But now Emiliano beat him at his own game. It was the baddest news Morgan had ever heard.

Emiliano said, "We haven't got time for that shit."

He was looking down, checking his gun. Directing the muzzle away from them he touched off a casual burst as if to test the weapon. It rang through the caves, a clattering din echoing deep within the mountain. A noise to wake the dead.

It was now or never, Morgan thought. The only place where they stood a chance was that big dark tunnel on the other side of the cave. It seemed to go on quite a ways. He would have to shove Emiliano and grab Page, and they would have to make a dash for it.

He was about to spring when Emiliano reached over and took hold of the strap of the camera hanging from Page's neck.

"Give it here," he said, jerking the strap.

Instinctively Page pulled away, grabbing the camera. It was her camera. He had no right to take it. Holding onto the strap Emiliano swept the back of his hand savagely across her face.

"You little bitch, give it here or I'll shove this up your cunt and pull the trigger!"

She let out a cry, her hand flying to her face, and Morgan felt a congealed rage, knowing there was nothing he could do while Chucho had him covered.

"You better give it to him," he told her.

Crying, her upper lip tasting of blood and already beginning to swell, she lowered her head and lifted the strap over, and Emiliano took the camera. One moment he was examining it, holding it up in his hand, the next it fell and struck the ground. In the same instant the cave began to tremble as if the falling camera had set off a cataclysm.

Morgan had experienced this once before and coincidentally it was in the same country. He had been in Caracas, traveling through, and was being entertained by an old friend who was the local bureau chief for one of the wire services. The friend was a hi-fi freak, and while they were having a drink in his apartment that evening before going out on the town, he had been putting a Beatles album on tape. He had borrowed the album from an acquaintance and would return it after taping it. He saved a lot on records that way.

The album was being taped when the trembling began. The needle screeched across the record and as if by magic a crack slithered up the white plaster wall. There was no time to turn off the phonograph or the tape recorder. Morgan and his friend rushed out of the apartment and down the stairs three flights, the elevator being a risky exit under the circumstances.

Outside they saw it all: splitting sidewalks, people pouring out of buildings, some of the buildings collapsing. The trembling lasted less than a minute but in that time the death and destruction throughout the city were enormous. As a testament to their vulturous trade Morgan and his friend hurried downtown to get the bad news out to the rest of the world for the latest broadcasts and editions.

However, there are other, shrewder vultures. For a small sum a local entrepreneur purchased from Morgan's friend the roll of tape that had been recording when the disaster occurred. He made it into a record that was sold as a curiosity item. The record, to anyone who didn't know what was happening, sounded strange. Certainly you couldn't dance to it. It commenced with Paul McCartney singing "Eleanor Rigby," went on to what sounded like an approaching subway train and then with a screech switched to Ringo Starr singing "Yellow Submarine," still with the subway train, louder and nearer than before, in the background.

This unusual performance was clarified by the title on the record. It said: Caracas Earthquake, 1967.

So now Morgan wasn't startled, he was delighted. The whole mountain was shaking with a welling rumble. In the split second that Emiliano and Chucho gaped in surprise he lunged, shoving the bigger man so that he stumbled back crashing into the smaller. He didn't have to grab Page. She had already bolted and they were both running back across the cave.

Now time, which had been going so fast, reversed itself. The dark tunnel seemed far away and he didn't think they would make it. It was like playing a record at a slower speed than it was recorded, the singer sounding as if he were suffering from a terminal disease, each word a trial to pronounce. "Doooon't cryyyy myyyy loooove . . ." Or like instant replay on the television: the play you had just seen at normal speed repeated in slow motion so that each clod of dirt kicked up by the players' spikes rose floating interminably in a languorous ballet.

About halfway across the cave he actually saw flying clods of dirt and realized he and Page were being shot at. He couldn't hear the gunfire because of the rumble. The mountain was shaking out of control and the white stones that carpeted the cave floor were bouncing like grease on a skillet. He expected at any moment to be hit by bullets or see Page stagger, but the shots were going wild. It was like hunting grouse or pheasant. The bird that took off right beneath your foot, startling you, was always harder to hit than the one that leaped up several yards ahead. The trembling of the mountain, the shove, had thrown Emiliano and Chucho off. But still time was going slowly and

Morgan felt as if he were wearing heavy boots and running through quicksand. Then the tunnel was before them, huge and dark, and as they dashed into it he allowed himself a single glance back and saw the hunters on the other side of the cave just beginning to realize that their birds were out of range.

"What's happening?" Page gasped out of breath.

"Earthquake!"

He grabbed her hand and they groped forward along the wall on their left. It was pitch black and he couldn't see. He wanted to get as far as he could before Emiliano and Chucho started spraying the tunnel. But he had begun to worry about falling rocks. The earthquake hadn't let up. Ordinarily they didn't go on this long. But that was probably time's fault too. It only seemed long because time had been going so slowly. Still it was strange. Frightening. This earthquake was not only continuing, it was getting worse, rising in intensity. He had a sudden vision of the tunnel collapsing on them that made him stop short, aghast, caught between the frying pan of a firing squad and the fire of burial alive.

"Christ! The whole bloody mountain is going to come down!"

There was something else, too. He knew from experience what an earthquake sounded like. It sounded like Ringo Starr singing in a subway station. If he had heard the strains of "Yellow Submarine" he might have been surprised, but it wouldn't have been entirely unprecedented. He wasn't about to accept the idea of an earthquake that smelled. Yet there it was, a perceptible odor growing stronger as the rumbling and shaking increased. He had never smelled anything quite like it. Mossy, dank . . . he searched for the right word as he stood holding onto Page, trying to decide between the fire or the frying pan.

"What's wrong?" she asked.

Oozy, rich, foul . . . primordial. Suddenly he chose the frying pan.

"Come on, let's get out of here!"

He turned and began to drag her back out of the tunnel.

"We'll be shot!" she cried.

He didn't answer, he didn't pause to explain. He felt as if the darkness was a wave bearing down upon them. Or maybe it was Time itself, embodied this time and with a capital T, contrary and willful as always. First it had gone fast. Then slow. Now it was faster than ever, the singer's voice rising into a maniacal falsetto.

As they emerged from the tunnel he saw Emiliano and Chucho ahead of them. They were approaching at a trot. Page tried to pull away from him but he held onto her. The wave was almost upon them and Morgan ran with a certainty that it was about to come crashing over their heads, a huge, formless mass shaping itself by its impending invisible attributes into a distinct and terrible presence, covered with dung and jungle rot and filled with teeth.

Emiliano and Chucho came to an abrupt halt, astonished to see their prisoners fleeing back to them. Immediately their machine guns came up and then something happened. Morgan liked to think in retrospect that his first sight of Cuyakiare was the look on Emiliano's face. The machine guns that had been leveled at them jerked up, firing over their heads, and now Morgan felt Page struggling to pull away from him.

"Let go! They're going to shoot us!"

In that instant, trying to hang onto her, he glanced over his shoulder and the look on his face must have gotten through to her. She turned and saw what he saw and screamed.

Cuyakiare loomed over them, his jaws descending so close that Morgan could feel the hot blast of his breath and the dripping moisture from his teeth. Then the jaws recoiled from the sting of machine gun bullets and Cuyakiare reared back with a roar.

Morgan dragged Page out from under and ran pulling her to safety. He turned and saw Emiliano firing at the animal.

"It's a tyrannosaur!" Page said. "It's him!"

They had fled to the right, toward the opening opposite the entrance where their climbing equipment was. They hadn't had time to choose their direction and now Cuyakiare stood between them and escape.

He rose like a skyscraper, rearing back on his hind legs beneath the dome of the ceiling. Morgan saw that he was made up of parts that didn't seem to go together. The tail had a life of its own. It was huge and powerful. The hind legs were those of an elephant. They supported an elephant's body. The forelegs were puny talons, meant for grasping prey. But there was nothing puny about the head. It was a formidable, ferocious machine. The teeth resembled stalactites and stalagmites. For a moment this absurd and frightening conglomeration rose and hung there like a towering edifice. Gothic architecture, Morgan thought. Then the entire structure seemed to topple forward, falling toward Emiliano.

Emiliano was proud of his legendary cool. He had once been burst in upon by French agents while he was making love in an apartment in the Latin Quarter. An informer had led them there and it was only the creak of their footsteps outside in the hall that had warned him. As the agents kicked in the door and opened fire he rolled off his girl friend and she was caught in it, lying naked on the bed, flopping up and down with bright red spots sprouting all over her. By the time they realized they had the wrong person, Emiliano had found his gun. He was drunk, he was naked, he had been taken by surprise, and he expected to die. Nevertheless he proceeded with deliberation, taking each agent one at a time, killing two and badly wounding the third. He was even able to catch the informer before he made it down the stairs and send him crashing into the wall at the bottom with a bullet in the back of his head.

So now he stood his ground, even though this thing he was facing made him feel more naked than he had ever felt in his life.

When it had first emerged from the tunnel he had fired at it wildly, causing it to rear back shaking its head, its tail thrashing and its forelegs held limply, like those of a kangaroo. But he shouldn't have rushed his shot. That was what the agents had done and the reason two of them were dead.

He fired again but this time he took aim at the exposed throat. The throat resembled the view he had had of the Autana when the helicopter had come in for a landing the other day: a gigantic stalk, craggy and seamed, at the base of which the jungle washed in, climbing part way up the sheer walls. Emiliano's bullets thunked into the soft, scaly, gray-green reptilian folds, raising puffs of dust, and the head snapped around, cocking an eye downward.

As the eye found Emiliano a chilling look came into it that reminded him of the time the llama had spit in his face when he was a boy. His father had taken him to an outdoor zoo where most of the animals were allowed to roam free. The llama had spied him from across the lawn and started toward him. At first Emiliano had thought nothing of it. It seemed impossible to him that an animal he didn't even know would take it into its head to express an opinion of him without provocation. But as the llama came up he saw the look in its eye: a look of unmistakable malevolence. It told Emiliano that he wasn't universally loved. Before he could retreat, however, the llama spat in his face.

Now it was the same look that came into Cuyakiare's eye. Emiliano even smelled a similar odor, the repugnant odor of llama spit. With a howl the animal fell toward him, staggering into a kind of lumbering waddle with its tail extended behind it to keep it from toppling over completely.

The head was low now and, backing away, Emiliano placed a burst between its eyes, hoping to penetrate the skull. He heard Chucho's gun chattering behind him and gave a quick glance over his shoulder, before turning back.

The angle was too high now for a brain shot so he sent a burst into the abdomen, raking it up and down from chest to belly, searching for a vulnerable spot, his Magdanich jerking in his hands until the clip ran dry and it was too late to shove another in.

The face loomed down, the great, round, unblinking brown eyes, the gaping jaws and bared teeth. He saw specks of blood on the cheeks where his bullets had hit, welling minute and bright as pinpricks, and apparently as harmless, and there was something else too, something that made him pause even under the circumstances: a cluster of white feathers hanging beneath the right eye like an interrupted tear, attached to the dangling wooden needle of a dart. But he didn't have time to wonder about it. He was busy fending off the face.

His hand went for the right nostril, grasping it with his thumb hooked on the inside. He raised his gun by the barrel and batted the animal on the nose. The hollow stock of the Magdanich was too light. He struck the nose once, twice ineffectually, like striking an automobile tire, holding the face away and then as it bore down on him, releasing the nostril and attempting to skip back.

Cuyakiare's right foreleg shot out and seized his ankle. From a distance the forelegs had seemed tiny. Up close their use became apparent: spindly, sinewy arms at the ends of which were talons as large as a toucan's beak. Grasping Emiliano's leg the talons snipped through the ankle. The left foot waggled a moment and then dropped off, and Emiliano gazed in dreamlike astonishment and disbelief at his foot, still in its shoe and bloody blue nylon sock, lying on the cave floor. He flung a look back at Chucho as if to confirm his impression that the foot was irrevocably lost and saw Chucho gaping helplessly, unable to fire now without hitting him.

The jaws widened and turning back Emiliano grabbed one of the upper teeth, balancing on his one foot. The tooth was hard to get a grip on, fat and slimy, but he dug his fingers into the gray fleshy gum and got them around the base. Hanging on, and proceeding with the same deliberation as when the agents had burst in on him, he raised the Magdanich in his free arm and brought it down on Cuyakiare's right eye. The stock bounced back as if the eyeball were a rubber beach toy. The eye didn't even water: a serene pool of malevolence.

Emiliano had time to raise his arm once more but not enough to bring it down before the mouth engulfed him and even then, even as he felt the jaws crushing the breath from his lungs and the teeth cracking his thighs, he continued to struggle, clawing and screaming, an odor of decaying food particles clogging his nostrils as the rough-textured tongue separated the upper part of his body from the splintered thighs and guided it back headfirst down the dark, moist, suffocating throat.

Page turned away and Morgan held her to him. He saw Cuyakiare rise again, like the successive stages of a skyscraper going up and up, Emiliano's legs dangling from his mouth. But he hung there only a moment before toppling forward into his lumbering charge. Chucho was firing at him and as Cuyakiare went after him the way was clear to the entrance.

"Hurry!" Morgan said. "Rig the rope the way I showed you."

"Where are you going?"

"I've got to get Karim."

He turned, cursing. He knew he shouldn't be doing this. He should be saving himself and Page. But Karim knew who was going to assassinate the king and Morgan had to find out.

Karim was in the alcove. He had rushed out when he heard Cuyakiare and then fled back. Now he was standing, frozen with fear, feeling as if he were in a bad dream.

He was thinking of what Morgan had said to him about losing his head. The remark had had a special significance for him. When he was a boy his father had taken him on a hunt in the desert. While they were there the chief of a nearby tribe had invited them to attend an execution in the village, which was actually no more than a collection of goatskin tents. A man was being executed for murder. The man was brought out and made to kneel with his hands tied behind him. As his body slumped over, with the bloody stump of its neck where once had been the head—which now lay in the dirt—Karim had achieved an erection. It told him something about himself.

Years later when he was in Beirut on government business, the episode had had its logical outcome. He bought a boy from a pimp for sexual purposes and paid a very high price for him because of what he intended to do and the need for absolute secrecy. In a small dingy room somewhere in the city, as he was reaching a climax he took a knife and slit the boy's throat. He then returned home having successfully completed his business.

So now as Morgan rushed in and grabbed him, Karim cried, "I won't go back! They'll have my head!"

He tried to pull away but Morgan was too strong for him.

"Would you rather spend the night with *that?*"

In the main cave they heard Cuyakiare roaring and the rattle of Chucho's machine gun. Morgan wrestled Karim out of the alcove and dragged him along the passageway. He could tell Cuyakiare was moving. Each footfall sent a shudder through the mountain. He had the same sensation as when he arrived late for a soccer match. Going through the tunnel that led into the stadium you could hear the roar of the crowd rising and falling like a strong wind, and then you were out of the tunnel and the roar was all around you.

He emerged from the passageway and saw Cuyakiare chasing Chucho. It was like a whirlpool, a counterpart of the awesome natural force that had created the cave ages ago, carving it out with an incredible swirling violence. Morgan stopped, hanging on to Karim, who struggled to pull away. Across the cave at the entrance Page was rigging up the rappel rope but he couldn't get to her. Too much was happening.

Chucho had tried to reach the small tunnels at the far end but he had been overtaken. He spun and started back and Cuyakiare swung around, his tail sending a barrage of white stones crackling against the walls. Halfway across the cave Chucho spun again and once more Cuyakiare went after him, his tail sweeping up a hail of stones. This time he caught up with him. Chucho turned and struck him on the face with his machine gun. Then one of the talons had him by the throat, lifting him kicking into the air. The Magdanich fell, falling as if dropped from a ten-story building. As he hung there, red in the face, and clutching at the talons, Cuyakiare raised a hind leg and drew a toenail down his breastbone, opening him up from neck to groin before taking him in his mouth.

Seeing this, Karim ceased struggling and let himself be dragged across the cave. Page was waiting for them. She had looped the rope over a knob of rock and the ends hung down to a ledge she had noted that morning.

Morgan took the rope. There was a sling attached to it and he thrust it at Karim. "Get this on."

Karim gaped down at the jungle, 1,600 feet below. He was afraid of heights. Three days ago when he was lowered to the caves he had been in agony.

"I can't! I don't know how!" But he took the sling and stepped into it and Morgan guided him back, giving instructions.

"Rope over the shoulder. Use this hand to control it. Lean right out."

Glancing over his shoulder Karim felt a familiar urge: a demon in his entrails coaxing him to leap. He hesitated.

"Over, damn you!" Morgan said and gave him a shove.

Karim stumbled back into space with a gasp and hung onto the rope. Then he began to shoot down it as Morgan had told him. He descended in panicky spurts, stop-start, stop-start, twirling, banging against the wall, until nearing the ledge he saw to his horror that the rope was several yards short. He would have to jump the rest of the way.

The jungle was spread out below green and shimmering, beckoning him sinisterly, a glint of river winding through it. He felt as if it were trying to absorb him, make him a part of the glare and stillness and remote cries of guacamayas and toucans drifting up. The demon in his entrails whispered.

"Jump, dammit!" Morgan shouted from above.

As Karim dropped off the end of the rope, an image flashed through his mind: the executioner's sword descending. He landed with one foot on the ledge, a sort of compromise. Grasping at air he toppled off and sailed screaming all the way down.

Morgan had seen climbers fall before and he found it an unsettling visual phenomenon. One moment the climber was as big as life and you saw every whisker on his face. The next he was retreating from you at an incredible rate, his body suddenly no bigger than a single whisker. But Morgan didn't have time to appreciate this. He was already reaching for the rope and turning to hand it to Page.

Then his mouth dropped open. She wasn't there. She was running back into the cave.

"What the hell, where—"

Morgan felt as if he had entered some realm of impossibility. It was as if Page had been in league with Cuyakiare all along and they had dreamed up this performance to show him how insubstantial his idea of reality was: that hard-nosed reliance on the facts that ultimately reduced everything to the precise rectilinear borders of a news story. He started after her, feeling he was violating not only his will but his sanity as well, following her back into the primordial smell and terrific roar.

Cuyakiare must have been surprised, he thought, which was probably why he just sat there and watched her coming. Surprised that any creature would approach him without apparent fear or the illusion of invulnerability that the stinging weapons had given to the other two. He who had never seen anything that wasn't afraid of him, who was undisputed ruler of his world and whose ancestors had ruled it before him. More than surprised: astonished that any creature could ignore a state of affairs that had prevailed for more than two hundred million years. Then again, maybe he was just digesting his food. Whatever, he made no move but sat back chewing and swallowing, as Page raced beneath his colossal knees, snatched up the camera which Emiliano had dropped on the ground, and raced back.

Now he moved but it was simply a flourish. Flicking his tail he lifted his head and emitted a howl that shook the air. Page turned, pivoting, raised the camera to her face. Click. Cock. Click. Two pictures before Morgan caught up with her and dragged her away.

The animal followed them to the cave's mouth with an appetite-sated curiosity. They were over the edge in an instant. His face loomed down toward the ledge they had descended to, below him and out of reach. The camera was still clicking and Cuyakiare offered a smile of sorts, showing his teeth between which like so many minute particles of meat were stuck the twisted machine gun and shreds of clothes from his recent meal.

Then with a final howl and a blast of his rank breath he went back into the cave.

Endangered Species

16

Joaquín thought he heard thunder and he looked up toward the Autana. There were no rain clouds sailing in over the top and he was about to resume hunting when he saw a tiny figure go over the overhang at the mouth of the cave and slide a short way down like a spider on a web before dropping off and falling all the way down as if the web had broken.

He marked where the body fell and waited, watching for the second figure he expected.

Just then two others came over the overhang and this time the web held. In the next instant the mouth of the cave was filled with movement, a vision so extraordinary that the minute it vanished Joaquín began to doubt his eyes.

His eyes hadn't lied about one thing, though. This morning he had seen two people reach the top of the Autana and rappel down to the cave. Now two were descending the mountain. Who was the one who had fallen?

He went in search of the body. The foot of the mountain was thick with jungle and it was hard going, hacking through it with his machete. For all he knew, the body had landed in a tree and they would have to wait for the vultures to discover it.

Late in the afternoon he finally found it lying on the ground, face down, looking like a discarded sack of nothing very substantial. Thank God, he thought. It wasn't Morgan or Page.

But who was it then? A man wearing a custom-tailored suit with a paperback book and two ballpoint pens in his pockets. The book and the pens had survived the fall in better shape than either the suit or the man. Joaquín hoisted him onto his shoulder and carried him back to camp. He was there, wrapping the body in his hammock when Morgan and Page arrived.

He looked up from his bundle. "Who is he?" he said.

"Prince Mabruk al-Karim of El Hajjaz," Morgan said.

"The one you said was kidnapped?"

"There's more to it than that. I'll tell you on the way. They're going to assassinate the King tomorrow morning in Caracas. How long will it take to get back to the village?"

"The current will be with us. I'd say between six and eight hours."

"Where are the others?"

"They went back to the river yesterday. They're waiting for us." Joaquín rose. He looked at them. He saw they were both exhausted. "So he was up there," he said.

Morgan knew he wasn't referring to Mabruk. "You saw him?" he said.

"When he stuck his head out the cave."

"It was him, all right. We've got pictures. I should say Page has pictures. She almost dove down his throat to get them."

Joaquín had grown up hearing the stories told by the men of the tribe but he had eventually become too old to believe in them. Now he felt like a child again.

"You found your dinosaur," he said to Page.

She smiled wearily. "I can hardly believe it."

"We better hurry," Morgan said. "It's an hour and a half back to the river. Do you think you can make it?" he asked her.

She drew a breath. "Lead the way."

They started out and Page had to force herself to keep going. Morgan was carrying their equipment and Joaquín had Karim in the hammock and all she had to carry was herself. But her whole body had become an unbearable burden.

She had gotten down the Autana all right. In fact, at first she had been gripped by a kind of hysterical excitement and was laughing and talking so much that Morgan had to warn her to calm down.

"It's not going to be easy getting off this thing."

On the third rappel she had found him going through the motions with unusual deliberation. She noticed his drawn face and the meticulous way he was threading a three-foot-long nylon tape through the hole in the end of his hammer and tying it to his harness. It was already attached by a lanyard.

"Dropping this doesn't bear thinking about," he said, at the same time making sure his bolt pouch was closed and secure.

Suddenly she understood the strain he was under. If the hammer or any other equipment fell their only choice would be to hang on the mountain and starve or cut the rope and get it over with. It sobered her up and she became absorbed in the difficulty of the descent: down, down, sometimes rappelling straight down a hundred and fifty feet to a minuscule ledge with nothing but the jungle below.

In the beginning she seemed to have mastered the steady controlled speed necessary for descent. But inevitably, as her hands became raw and cramped and weariness overtook her, she made mistakes. Toward the end, coming over an overhang she failed to brake herself and plummeted, hitting a ledge and bouncing off. But in the split second halt she managed to pull the rope tight across her back and stop the plunge. She reached Morgan under control, shaken but smiling.

"I used everything on that one except my teeth."

Morgan had some unexpected news that wiped the smile from her face. "We've run out of bolts," he said. "We're still about three hundred feet from the ground and there's only one left. We'll have to tie our ropes together and hope they do the trick."

He knotted the ropes and lowered them but it was impossible to tell if they worked. A leap of fifty feet, even thirty, Page knew, could be fatal.

"When you're halfway down," he told her, "you'll have to work the knot through the brake bar. Hang from a jumar while you do it."

"But what if the ropes aren't long enough?"

"If you hear me whistle it means come down even if my weight isn't off the rope. We might be able to make a chain with our slings and harnesses to give us a few more feet."

He started down and minutes later Page felt his weight come off the rope. He was below a bulge in the rock and she assumed he had reached the ground.

When she came to the end of the joined ropes, however, she saw he hadn't. She was fifteen feet from the treetops and eighty feet off the ground. She looked around and called in alarm, "Where are you? What should I do?"

The top of the tree beneath her was flailing about and a voice rose from among the leaves. "Kick off and drop into this. Don't miss or you're dead."

The tone was hard and she knew it was to make her understand she only had one chance. She took two steps sideways to be directly over the tree, then doubled her legs, pushed off from the rock and gave a short sob as she let go of the rope.

The fall was silent and the crash and crackle of her landing deafening. Branches tore at her flesh and clothes and pummeled her back and ribs. She felt two hands grab her harness and she came to a halt. She opened her eyes and saw Morgan's white face. He shook her almost angrily.

"I thought you'd overshot the damn tree. If you had, you'd be done for."

"Hell David," she said, "when you take people climbing you really take them climbing."

He pointed down. "Get going monkey."

They climbed carefully down the frail upper branches until they reached solid limbs and the main trunk, then slid fifty feet to the ground. Page sat down. Then she lay down.

"Let me feel the horizontal world for a moment," she pleaded.

But now, heading back to the river, she had to keep going. She was dying for this hour and a half to be over with. Each step was painful. She tried to ignore the pain, she told herself it was necessary, a good pain because it was bringing her closer to where she could lie down. She kept telling herself that an hour and a half really wasn't so long, it was only ninety minutes, only about as long as it would take her to get ready to go out to dinner with John if she was in no mood to hurry: An hour and a half really wasn't enough time to do anything. But somehow she couldn't imagine herself on the other side of it.

It was dusk when they reached the river and she was too tired to care about anything. She wasn't even interested in asking what José and the two brothers said when Joaquín told them that the bundle over his shoulder was a dead man. She let Morgan guide her to a place in the middle of the *curiara* and she lay down and curled up and was only dimly aware when they shoved off.

Once she woke and they were gliding down a long, dark corridor of trees with a moonlit sky above. She heard the motor buzzing steadily, and breathing the cool, sweet night air she went back to sleep. Another time the *curiara* was stopped and the men were trying to work it through a difficult spot and she knew she should get out and help but how could she do that if she was already asleep again.

Then Morgan was bending over her in the dark. He was standing outside the *curiara*.

"You awake?"

"Yes, are we here?"

"You slept straight through. Here, have some of this."

The *curiara* was pulled up on the riverbank. Page sat up and took the tin cup of coffee he handed her along with something to eat.

"What is it?"

"A pancake."

She sipped the coffee and tried the pancake. There was sugar on it and she realized how hungry she was.

"Mm, these are good."

"We've got more in the plane. We're already loaded. Joaquín's going to fly us. I'm a little groggy."

Morgan helped her out.

"My God, I'm stiff. I slept like a log. What time is it?"

"Almost morning."

"Are we in time to save the King?"

"I think so."

They went through the village. Here and there a lantern glowed inside a hut and dogs barked at them as they passed. Somewhere a cock crowed. They came out into the open and the plane was at one end of the landing strip warming up, while a group of tribesmen stood watching. There was a slight chill in the air and the sky was beginning to lighten above the black circle of trees.

"I didn't know Joaquín could fly a plane."

"He probably learned to fly before he could walk. His mother taught him."

They approached the plane and Page recognized the chief standing with his arms folded. Morgan spoke to him above the noise of the engine and the chief unfolded one of his arms and touched him on the shoulder. Morgan helped her into the plane, holding open the door on the passenger side.

"You'll have to get in back. I've got to use the radio."

Page climbed in and Joaquín turned to her from the pilot's seat. He had exchanged his *guayuco* for a pair of dungarees and a sport shirt. "Morning. How you feel?"

"I'm still half asleep. You and David have been up all night. You must be exhausted."

Morgan climbed in and closed the door. "Buckle up."

Page fastened her seat belt. There was a large bundle next to her and Joaquín's blowpipe lay across the backs of the seats the entire length of the cabin.

The engine began to roar and the plane shook. Morgan raised his hand to the chief and they began to roll forward, bouncing along the rutted strip and gaining speed. As they reached the steep hump two-thirds of the way down, the plane lifted off into the lightening sky, just clearing the fringe of trees. They rose higher and Page looked out, sipping her coffee and eating another pancake. The sun was beginning to come up. The plane dipped to the right and there was the river and the scattered fires of the village in the endless sweep of jungle.

At the same instant the bundle in the next seat fell over against her and pushing it back, she realized with a certain consternation that it was the dead man in the hammock.

"Kilo Tango Fox to Ciudad Bolívar control. Do you read me? Over."

Morgan was trying to contact the air traffic controller at Ciudad Bolívar, which was the first town after the jungle. He felt no urgency now. The urgency had been before when he had known that in the time it would take them to reach the village, traveling by night on a river with the current behind them and their outboard motor racing, anything might go wrong.

For a while they had had the moon overhead. Then it had gone down behind the trees and the river was pitch black, and they had had to depend on José's knowledge of its rapids and shallows.

Morgan hadn't slept for twenty-four hours. But he would be able to as soon as he could get the air traffic controller to warn the authorities.

He tried again. "Kilo Tango Fox to Ciudad Bolívar control. Do you read me? Over."

The radio bristled with static as a voice came on. They both spoke Spanish.

"Ciudad Bolívar to Kilo Tango Fox. Go ahead."

"This is very important," Morgan said. "The King of El Hajjaz is in Caracas. He's going to be assassinated this morning at a meeting at the Banco Central. You've got to warn the police. Do you read me? Over."

Static. The voice sounded as disgusted as a disembodied voice could.

"Jesus, here we go again. Why is it I have to put up with every drunk who thinks he can fly a plane? Who the hell let you up?"

The static ceased, the voice gone without bothering to ask if it had been heard or even to sign off with an "over."

"I'm not drunk. I'm dead serious. The King is going to be assassinated. Do you read me?"

After a pause the voice came on as if from an afterthought.

"We don't have any kings in this country. The politicians are bad enough."

"This is the King of El Hajjaz. He's visiting Venezuela. His nephew was kidnapped the other day. It was in all the newspapers."

"I haven't got time to read the newspapers. I'm too busy listening to guys like you."

"But this is the truth."

There was no answer. Morgan was about to try again when the static crackled and the voice said, "Where are you?"

At last, Morgan thought. He spoke slowly and deliberately.

"I am a hundred and seventy-five miles south of Ciudad Bolívar. I have been in the village of the Makiritare. I am heading for Caracas. Please notify the police that the King is going to be assassinated at the Banco Central this morning."

"I get it. You've been with the Makiritare. Who told you all this? An alligator?"

"I'm not joking."

"I'm not joking either," the voice said sharply. "If you don't get off the air I'll report you." Click. Out.

Morgan tried to get the controller back. "Ciudad Bolívar, this is Kilo Tango Fox. Do you read me? Do you read me, Ciudad Bolívar?"

There was no response. He continued to try and then the radio settled the matter by going dead. He swore at the fact that the plane had only one transmitter.

"What do you think?" Joaquín said.

"I guess we'll have to wait till we get to Caracas. There's still plenty of time before the meeting starts."

As soon as they landed Morgan would telephone the Interior Minister. Of course it would help if he could tell him who was bringing the bomb into the negotiating room. But there weren't that many who would be allowed in the room. He had determined their number and identity when he first arrived in Caracas to cover the loan story. Besides the King—and Karim, who had arranged to be absent—the only others were the president of the Central Bank, his two assistants and the King's aide, Asaad Shaaban.

Shaaban was the logical choice. Karim would have had ample opportunity to enlist him back home. But, on the other hand, Emiliano might have handled it and Morgan now recalled something the public relations director at the bank had told him about one of the president's assistants. He had made a joke of it: How ironic it was that someone working in a bank, a rising executive no less, should have once been dedicated to the overthrow of capitalism. Amusing, no? Everyone knew about it and no one held it against him. It had been a long time ago when the assistant had been a student at the University. He had served as a courier between the revolutionaries in the city and the guerrillas in the mountains. Since then the fellow had been converted to the capitalistic system by the usual means of having found a good job. But his conversion, Morgan realized, needn't be as genuine as it seemed.

One thing was clear. The assassin intended to escape. He was no fanatic willing to sacrifice his life. That's why they had come to Venezuela and were using a time bomb in a closed room. A time bomb would allow him to get away. El Hajjaz was a small country whose borders were easily patrolled. The risk was greater there, and if the assassin was captured he might tell who had put him up to it, something Karim would have wanted to avoid at all cost. Here in Venezuela you had the whole jungle to disappear in, and a man could lie low for as long as was necessary, fortified by the knowledge that he was being taken care of handsomely.

When Karim was found alive, with Jules Smith released and in Libya to make Karim's reappearance "look right," he would simply be regarded as a luckier victim of the men who had killed his uncle.

If Morgan had only let Karim finish his joke: *"These* mules are going to be too much for the King." That was the key. But he had been angry and at the time he hadn't thought it would do either him or the King any good. Now the secret was safe with the body in the hammock.

So Morgan didn't know who the assassin was but he had a sudden vision of how it would happen. A man would enter the bank and he wouldn't be stopped or searched because he was somebody who belonged there. He would go into the negotiating room, where he would leave his package next to the King. The package might be as large as an attaché case or as small, considering the way they were making them these days, as the watch Morgan was drawing from his pocket. As the meeting was about to begin, the man would discover that he had to take a pee or that he had forgotten to ask his wife to send his dress suit to the dry cleaners. They might even laugh about it. He would go off to take a pee or phone his wife and instead he would leave the building and get into a car that was waiting for him several blocks away.

Morgan thought of the King as he knew him, with his shrewd merry eyes that saw so clearly. Then he saw the clear-seeing eyes torn from their sockets by the bomb blast. He flipped open his watch.

"We should be there more than an hour before the meeting."

Snapped the lid shut. Put the watch back in his pocket. He was worried but confident. He even allowed himself to doze off. The doze lasted only a moment. The next thing he knew Joaquín was shaking him by the shoulder.

"Jesus, David, we're losing oil fast! We must have a leak!"

Morgan jerked awake. The needle on the oil gauge was down in the yellow quadrant and they were already losing altitude. He cursed the fate that had arranged for him to rent a plane with only a single radio transmitter and the potential for an oil leak. They would never get to Caracas in it.

The mechanic at El Buitre's jungle airstrip didn't know what to make of it. It's early morning and he's having his coffee and this small plane lands and taxies up to his workshop near the runway and before the prop stops spinning a man jumps out and rushes up to him.

They're in a hurry, he says, they have to get to Caracas.

"Okay, okay," the mechanic says, "take it easy, hombre. We got all day. The sun just came up."

No, the man says, they haven't got all day.

"Oh, yes you have," the mechanic says. "In this town you do."

Is there a radio in the airport, the man wants to know. Only the kind you get music out of, the mechanic says. The airport is just a field and a shack with a few barrels of gasoline and some tins of oil.

What about a telephone, are there any in town? The mechanic looks at him like he's crazy. You know why they call this town El Buitre? It's because the buzzards outnumber the humans.

So then the man drags him over to the plane and right away he sees that the fuselage is streaked with oil all the way back to the tail. This was before he sees who's flying the plane.

"You got problems, all right," he says. "You want to walk into town and get a bite to eat, something to drink? I'll see what I can do about it this afternoon."

"No," the man grabs him by the arm, "we haven't got time. You've got to fix it now."

Just then the pilot and the other passenger climb out. The passenger is a woman. She looks like she's been flying on the outside of the plane. The pilot is an Indian, which isn't so unusual. After all, next to buzzards what they got most of around here is Indians. Only the mechanic has never seen one flying a plane before.

Now he's beginning to worry. There's something suspicious about these three. Just last week a dead man had been found washed up on the riverbank outside of town. He was naked and his head had been cut off. The mechanic had seen him when the sheriff brought him in, and the sight of the dead man, with his bare buttocks over a mule's back and the obscene stump of neck dangling down, had horrified him. He thinks these people have something to do with it and he figures he better do as they say.

First he wipes the oil off and runs the engine full blast for twenty minutes, then he pokes around under the cowling, and all along he can hear the three of them talking about some person who's going to get killed and it makes him nervous. But it's nothing like what he feels when he gets a look at what's sitting in the back seat of the cabin. He sees this figure wrapped up in a hammock and he knows it's human because he can see the outline of its arms and legs and he's wondering what the hell would somebody be doing sitting in the back seat of a plane wrapped up in a hammock . . . and then it dawns on him, the man is dead.

Now the mechanic is really scared.

He tells them what's wrong. Oil is leaking from the forward portside cylinder through a broken gasket. Then he gives them the verdict he figures will get them to go into town after all, so he can hurry up and find the sheriff.

"*Ustedes salen en eso y se maten.* You go up in this and you're dead."

He figured that would scare the three of them—the fourth, it didn't look like it mattered much. But the first man just gives him a mean look.

"Tighten it," he says. "Just tighten it so we can get to Caracas."

"Well, I don't know," the mechanic says. "I can tighten it all right, only I don't have a torque wrench that'll fit a bolt that size, and the only guy in town who does is Antonio Ching, who owns a helicopter, and it's still pretty early, Antonio likes to sleep late, he stays up all night drinking rum and chasing pussy, and he can get pretty nasty if you wake him before——"

So all of a sudden he sees himself naked and headless on the riverbank because the man grabs him hard by the front of his shirt, clenching his teeth and saying, "Tighten it! Tighten it, you lying son of a bitch or you'll end up like that guy in the hammock that you've been sneaking looks at for the last ten minutes!"

17

King Jalal had spent a sleepless night, and as a result he was already sitting at his desk early next morning, going over papers that would prepare him for that day's resumption of the loan talks, when Shaaban rapped on the door and entered, bringing with him the familiar odor of his Lebanese cigarettes.

It was an odor that clung to Shaaban regardless of whether he was smoking or not, inhabiting his clothes and perhaps, the King often thought, even his skin. This morning was a case in point. He had no cigarette—in fact, the one thing the King insisted on was that his aide refrain from smoking until he, Jalal, had at least had breakfast—and yet the odor was there, as reliable as Shaaban's "Good morning, Your Majesty."

"Is there any news?" the King asked.

"No, sir. I telephoned Miraflores. They said they would notify you."

"Did they say when they thought they might hear something?"

"They hope it might be today. It was too soon for anything last night."

The King rose stiffly. "What time is it?"

"It's seven-thirty. The limousine will be here at a quarter to nine."

"I have some letters to dictate," the King said.

Shaaban took out a pad. Standing in his bathrobe before the windows, looking out at the bright new day, the King began to dictate.

His quarters at Los Cedros, the mansion reserved for visiting dignitaries and heads of state, overlooked a garden shaded with avocado, lemon and pomegranate trees. Flowering *trinitarias* discreetly concealed the barbed wire strung along the top of the wall surrounding the yard. Beyond, the King saw red flamboyants in the neighboring garden and, across the city to the south, the green hills of Prados del Este and El Peñon. But his eyes were too grainy from lack of sleep to enjoy the view.

Once during the night he had thought he heard voices coming down the hall outside his bedroom and had sat bolt upright expecting Shaaban to enter with news that Mabruk had been found. But it had just been his imagination and he had been left alone in the dark with his anxiety.

There had never been any doubt that the council of citizens would accede to his wishes in the matter of his nephew's kidnap, but it had to be allowed to express its opinion. Many of the older members disliked Mabruk and perhaps this had influenced their argument that it was wrong to bow to the demands of terrorists. Now, however, Jules Smith had been released and flown to Libya and there was nothing to do but wait.

The King tried to dictate letters without success. It was his habit to work before breakfast. At home he would rise at dawn and wouldn't eat until eight-thirty. He worked better on an empty stomach. But this morning his head was full of cobwebs and worry and he was having a hard time remembering what he meant to say.

Finally he admitted, "I've been awake all night. I kept thinking of Mabruk lying on some road, tied up and waiting for somebody to discover him."

"I'm sure he'll be all right," Shaaban said.

"Well, I suppose there's no use trying to finish this with my brain the way it is. It's getting time for the meeting."

After a day's delay the King had insisted that the loan talks continue. It was one of his tenets that a monarch owed it to his people never to let a personal tragedy interfere with his public duties. The talks had been resumed on Friday, adjourned for the weekend and today it was Monday.

"I'll have breakfast," he told Shaaban.

"Do you wish it in your room?"

"Yes, I'm going to shower."

Shaaban left but his odor remained. Actually, to the King, it wasn't an unpleasant odor. It reminded him of camel dung, a smell he was fond of. Otherwise he wouldn't have been so tolerant of his aide's smoking. He really should get him to give it up. It was bad for his health and it created a bad impression to have him always standing around at official functions puffing away like a steam engine, furtively clutching one of his Lebanese terrors between stained fingertips. But the King knew how hard it was to give up smoking, having gone through the ordeal as a young man, and he doubted his aide could manage it. Shaaban was an extremely nervous fellow and to deprive him of his habit . . . how was it the Americans put it, "cold turkey" . . . to do that would completely unhinge him. So the King contented himself with reminding him now and then that he should cut down on his number of packs a day and left it at that.

Odd expression, "cold turkey." He wondered at its derivation as he went into the bathroom to shower.

Oh, how he wished he were home and all this trouble were over, he thought, lifting his bearded face to the spray. That was the one good thing about Shaaban's odor. Camel dung. Whenever his aide was in the room all the King had to do to be transported to the desert was close his eyes.

He had been brought up as a child among the tribes and it was in the tribal black tents of the desert that he truly felt at home. He had even gone so far as to have tents set up on his palace grounds so that whenever he felt the need to escape the demands of protocol he had only to step out his back door and walk across the yard to spend an evening there, reclining on silken cushions, dining and talking with friends.

Mabruk often complained about how old-fashioned he was. But a man could not help where he had been born, and the saddest men were those who tried to deny their origins. All men, at one time or another, went through a period of denying their origins, the King supposed, and the attempt invariably produced grotesques. Like fat ladies trying to fit into tight clothes. He had sometimes sensed this about Mabruk, that he was a mechanical, unhappy man who had cut himself off from his roots. But he was sure his nephew would outgrow this and he hoped he was still alive to have the chance. In the meantime the King did not want his people to be ashamed of their desert ways because these ways were as old and durable as the desert itself.

By the time he had showered and dressed in his traditional robe, Shaaban had returned, holding the door open for a servant who wheeled in a table. The staff at Los Cedros had arranged to provide the King with his usual breakfast during his stay: Bedouin coffee flavored with cardamom and some flat cakes without butter or jam.

Shaaban stood by while the King ate and now, although there was still no cigarette in his hand, the desire was clearly upon him. He kept removing an unopened pack from his jacket pocket.

It was like the time the King had hired him years ago. Before then he had used the same aide that had served his father, an old man whom Jalal was fond of and couldn't bear to let go. But when the fellow died, the King had asked Mabruk to find him a new aide, this time young, educated and with a modern outlook. Several days later Shaaban had appeared for an interview. His credentials were excellent but even then the King could see he was a bundle of nerves, fidgeting and feeling his pockets until finally the King had said, "For God's sake, man, smoke. I'd rather have you smoking than picking at yourself like a monkey."

But now he wasn't so sure. It was time for Shaaban to show some will power before it was too late. He wondered how to broach the subject without being dictatorial.

"Cold turkey," he said, sipping his coffee.

"Your Majesty?"

"I was wondering where the expression 'cold turkey' comes from."

"It's an American bird. They serve it on a national holiday."

"No, that's hot turkey. They serve hot turkey on the holiday. 'Cold turkey' is a colloquial expression. I remember when I was in New York after the Second World War. I went to a show on Broadway, a musical entertainment, and while I was standing in the lobby during the intermission I overheard a man say, 'This is a real turkey.' He meant it was a bad show and he was right. It was terrible. If you want to say something is bad in America you say, 'It's a real turkey.' But now they have this 'cold turkey.' It means to give up something abruptly, usually applied to heroin addiction, I believe, but also used for other bad habits such as . . . smoking."

He looked up to see if his aide got the point but Shaaban only said, "Perhaps the bird served cold is unappetizing, an abrupt change from the feast of the day before," then glanced at his watch and added, "I better see if the limousine is here."

The King had finished his breakfast by the time his aide returned, and in anticipation of this Shaaban had an unlit cigarette in his mouth.

"The limousine is waiting," he said.

He held the door open and as the King started out he stopped and faced his aide earnestly.

"Cold turkey, Shaaban. I think it's time for you to give up smoking . . . cold turkey."

Shaaban smiled. This in itself was a rarity, since he was a solemn young man. So at least, the King thought, he was accepting the suggestion with good humor. On the other hand, Shaaban's smile wasn't something you looked forward to. His teeth, slightly crooked, were so tobacco-stained that one expected to smell bad breath. It was a smile that invariably reminded the King of death.

"You're right, Your Majesty, I've been meaning to give it up." He pulled a crumpled pack from his pocket. "This is my last pack today."

"What about that unopened one you've been fiddling with?"

Once more the smile, the impression of bad breath as Shaaban withdrew the unopened pack from his other pocket and held it up.

"My test of discipline," he said. "As long as I don't open it, I know I'm safe."

The brand was familiar to the King. He had seen it many times. The pack was bright yellow and blue. It was distinguished by a picture of a mule standing in the desert. The name of the cigarettes was Humara, which is the Arabic word for "mules."

18

The streets bounding three sides of the Plaza Bolívar in the heart of Caracas are always closed to traffic. As a result, coming from Carlota Airport the closest David Morgan could get to the Central Bank in his car was the south side of the plaza, which was about two blocks away.

Morgan had had to put the fear of God into the mechanic at El Buitre in order to get their plane off the ground, and when they had finally touched down at Carlota and taxied to Bay Five it was only minutes before the meeting was to begin at the bank.

"The car's in the parking lot," he said, handing the keys to Joaquín as he jumped out and headed for the terminal building.

He reached the building and looked inside and saw that the single phone was in use. He considered the amount of time he had wasted in his life waiting for telephones. The man might hang up immediately or he might go on for twenty minutes. Twenty minutes wouldn't be unusual, but in this case it was too long.

He hurried to the parking lot. Joaquín and Page were in the car. Morgan got in the driver's seat and sped out past the guard at the gate.

He hadn't bothered to pay for the rental of their plane or to explain about the body they were leaving behind in the cabin along with all their gear.

The traffic was what you would expect on a Monday morning. The chief means of mass transportation in Caracas is called a *"por puesto"*: an ordinary taxicab which, instead of collecting a single fare per trip, picks up as many passengers as it can, going the same way, each of whom pays a portion of the fare.

Now the streets were volatile with *por puestos* and Morgan tried to get through the snarl while Joaquín rode with his arm outside the window, carrying his blowpipe on the roof.

"They'll have every approach to the bank blocked off," Morgan said. "They don't want another kidnapping. If I can just get there before the King does. If I can just get him to *see* me . . ."

He swore, honking his horn at a sluggish cab.

At last they reached the Plaza Bolívar and could go no farther in the car. Morgan pulled up at the curb.

"We'll have to run." He and Joaquín got out. "Stay here," he told Page.

"I want to go," she said.

"There's nothing you can do. Either we're in time or it's too late."

He was already hurrying up the short flight of steps into the plaza with Joaquín. It was as if he had suddenly been transported back to the jungle: a pruned jungle, the islands of lovely overhanging trees intersected by paved walks radiating from a center in which stood a statue of Simón Bolívar, the Liberator of South America, on horseback. Morgan sprinted down one of the walks to the statue and without breaking stride continued on up another walk. The plaza's lone occupant, a man sitting on a folding chair reading a newspaper, glanced up as the two men hurtled by, one carrying a bamboo blowpipe and looking as if he had just come swinging down out of the surrounding trees. But Morgan didn't look back. He reached the other side and bounded up the steps out of the plaza.

Coming onto the street he saw, halfway up the next block, the police barricade he had expected. It was crowded with people. Beyond the barricade, at the end of the block, was the intersection with

Avenida Urdaneta where the bank was. To reach it they would have to get past the barricade. Morgan didn't pause. Heading up the street he gave a final burst of speed.

As he came up to the barricade out of breath, the people turned to him. They were there to see the King, although they would only catch a glimpse of him in a closed limousine as it passed half a block away. The fact that they were still there meant the King hadn't arrived yet.

Morgan pushed through them to one of the two policemen behind the barricade. The policeman was ignoring the people except to motion them back with his hand whenever they pressed forward too hard.

Morgan spoke to him. "Officer, I'm a newspaper reporter. I've been assigned to cover the loan talks. Can I get through here?"

Morgan wasn't worth wasting words on either. He got the same gesture as everyone else.

"I work for the London *Globe,*" he said.

The policeman turned and gripped the wooden plank of the barricade. "No one is allowed past," he said without looking at him.

On the left was a sunken plaza. Looking across it Morgan could see the bank plainly except for a tree that grew from a corner of the plaza, partly blocking the view with its spreading foliage. He caught the eye of the other policeman.

"What's the trouble?" this one said.

Morgan explained his problem again.

"Have you any identification?" the policeman said.

Morgan had been afraid of this question. "It's at my hotel. I've been out of town and I just got back. I came straight from the airport."

The first policeman faced him now. "You have no identification?" he said.

"I have identification but I left it with the desk clerk at the Tamanaco. I didn't need it where I was going."

"Where have you been?"

"In the jungle."

"What were you doing there?"

So here it comes, Morgan thought, the inquisition. The first policeman was scrutinizing him narrowly. He was a short man, more Indian than anything else, with a bony simian face and a savage glint in his eye.

"I was covering a story," Morgan said to the second one, a big beefy man with a mustache.

"What nationality are you?" the second asked.

"British. I work for the London *Globe.*"

"Oh yes, I've heard of it."

"I've got to get past," Morgan told him. "I have to cover this story."

"I'm afraid we can't let you past without identification."

"Have you got a passport?" the first said.

"It's at my hotel," Morgan said.

He knew it would do no good to lose his temper. The first policeman seemed to be smoldering with repressed rage.

"You realize it's against the law to be without identification?" he said. "You know there's been a kidnapping?"

"Leave him alone," the second said. "He's a British newspaper reporter."

"How do we know? He hasn't even had a shave."

Morgan was afraid to mention the word assassination because he was sure it would get him arrested. South American police weren't noted for their patience and the short one was clearly out for blood.

"This man could be anybody," he said. His nostrils flared as if at the unmistakable odor of evil. "It's like the other day. Everyone thought it was an ambulance outside the bank. Now you have all these soldiers to protect the King, and what for? No one has eyes to see."

Morgan was frantic, but he saw if he stayed longer he would be in trouble. The kidnapping had confirmed the first policeman's belief in a constant state of lawlessness against which he was the sole protector. Morgan shrugged, smiling at the second one.

"Bueno, señor. I guess I'll just have to go back to the Tamanaco for my press pass. Thank you anyway."

The second made an apologetic gesture and Morgan backed out of the crowd as unobtrusively as possible. The people were looking at him. "I do not believe he has identification," he heard the first saying.

Joaquín was standing at the edge of the crowd and Morgan stood with him trying to seem calm until the people stopped looking at him and resumed their festive and curious vigil for the King.

"It's no good," he said.

"We might make a run for it," Joaquín said indicating the sunken plaza.

Morgan's gaze traveled down the long flight of steps that led into the plaza. Below on the broad expanse of concrete he saw a few small potted trees, a lamppost, a litter basket. At the far end a fountain sent up plumes of water into a rectangular pool. The pool was fed by a man-made waterfall that came from spouts in the wall behind it. Above the high wall was Avenida Urdaneta and across the avenue was the bank.

The plaza was empty of people. A flock of pigeons was foraging on the pavement. Morgan saw a cat stalking them.

He considered the proposition only a moment. It was as if he were mesmerized by the splashing fountain and the watery cooing of pigeons, the morning peaceful, sunny, inviolable, something from which he had been temporarily removed and which he could contemplate with a kind of dreamy detachment as the cat crept up on the unwary birds and all around, like an undercurrent, came the remote hum of traffic and beep of horns.

Abruptly the horns became insistent and there was movement among the people at the barricade. Looking up he saw at the end of the block the limousine passing with the King in his headdress barely visible in the back.

"Come on," he said to Joaquín.

The police had their eyes on the King too. Still Morgan didn't hurry until he was halfway down the steps. Then with a leap down the bottom flight he broke into a run with Joaquín.

The cat spied them coming and faced them, crouched on its haunches, tail flicking in momentary indecision before it took off with a hiss of indignation and Morgan, plunging past, barreled in among the pigeons, loosing the entire flock as if he had detonated a bomb.

The birds erupted about him with a wild flapping, a metallic clatter rising and spreading in a kind of whirlpool of panic that stirred a gust and sucked up in its vortex an eddying flotsam of dust and molted feathers. They rose in a loose bunch that swung in a circle over the plaza high against the blue sky above the city, circling once, twice rapidly before coming together to land. It was like a pattern of buckshot spreading from a shotgun blast and then being sucked back into the barrel by motion-picture magic. The flock lit on the same spot it had lifted off from and instantly the cat was crouching to resume its interrupted stalk.

Morgan saw none of this, though the two policemen behind the barricade did. He was rushing for the wall. Now it was not only as if he were back in the jungle but as if he were at the foot of the Autana itself: the waterfall, the wall hung with vines and, rearing up behind it on the other side of the street, like a mountain of concrete and glass, the bank.

Only you don't have to climb it, he thought. There's no dinosaur up there. All you have to do is get to it before the King gets inside.

The wall rose in two stages. As he approached the first, next to the waterfall, Morgan assessed it in climbing terms: vegetation pitch. With a running leap along the raised rim of the pool he scrabbled at the vines that decorated the wall, pulling himself up and onto it. He turned and took the blowpipe that Joaquín handed up to him and turned back to consider the second stage as Joaquín scrambled up beside him.

This time he thought: jugs, bloody big ones too. The jugs were the four spouts from which water was pouring to feed the waterfall. Joaquín had a go at them. In a moment he was standing on them within reach of the iron railing that ran along the top of the wall. Grabbing the railing and kicking off from the spouts, he pulled himself up and over.

As Morgan handed the blowpipe up to him he saw the look on Joaquín's face and turned to see the two policemen running toward them across the plaza. Once more the pigeons exploded like flying shrapnel, rising and flapping and going into their circle above the plaza, twice around, before landing in the same spot. But Morgan didn't see this either. He was pulling himself up over the railing with Joaquín's help. Now they both stood facing the bank.

Instantly their hands went up. The sidewalk outside the bank was lined with soldiers: the extra guard that had been put on. The minute they saw the two men come over the railing they were alert.

Morgan hesitated. He knew if he rushed across the street he would be shot. The King had emerged from his limousine at the curb and was already halfway up the long broad flight of steps to the recessed entrance. Morgan had to get his attention without appearing to be a threat.

"Don't shoot!" he shouted.

He started across the street slowly with Joaquín, their hands raised. There was a stir among the soldiers.

"Don't shoot!"

The King didn't hear him. Or maybe he heard but thought nothing of it. Anyway he continued on up the steps without turning.

"El Rey!" Morgan shouted, pointing with one raised hand toward the retreating figure. "The King!"

The word, the title alone, was a provocation. The soldiers began to lower their rifles. The King had almost reached the entrance.

Then Morgan saw something. Shaaban had just started up the steps after having held the limousine door open for the King, and exchanged a word or two with one of the bank officials on the sidewalk. As he did so he took a final puff on his cigarette and tossed it in the gutter. It was an act that Morgan had witnessed before and it struck a barely conscious chord of memory. Shaaban the chain-smoker: his distinctive brand. Morgan saw the unopened pack in the aide's hand and he realized the ending of Mabruk's unfinished joke.

He gasped a single word: "Mules!" Then, turning to Joaquín and pointing wildly at Shaaban, he shouted, "It's the cigarettes! In his hand! The pack of cigarettes!" At the same instant he went for the soldiers.

He still didn't drop his hands, he wanted to give himself at least that chance for survival, holding them high and obviously harmless as he ran forward. The soldiers closed about him, attempting to restrain this madman, this suicidal assassin. In the confusion they completely forgot the other man, who was raising his blowpipe.

When they had taken off from the Makiritare village that morning, Page had asked Morgan why they were bringing the blowpipe.

"You never can tell," he had told her. "If we can't get a warning through, it might come in handy."

"But wouldn't it have been simpler to bring a gun?"

"The only gun in the village is a beat-up old shotgun. Have you ever tried to run down a street in a big city carrying a shotgun?"

Now Morgan relaxed a moment to give the soldiers a false sense of security before lunging upward again. Breaking loose above their heads he shouted back at Joaquín.

"The Mules! It's the Mules!"

As he ascended the steps, King Jalal had his mind on other things besides the commotion going on below. The first indication he had that something was wrong came from Shaaban. But even this, assuming the form it did, was misinterpreted.

His aide gasped. No, it was more than a gasp: a violent intake of air followed by a cry of . . . was it anguish, or did he simply want to get the King's attention?

There was Shaaban, four or five steps behind him, holding up his hand, attached to the palm of which, by a white feather it seemed, was the pack of cigarettes they had just been discussing a short time ago. For a moment the King was under the impression that his aide had chosen this unusual way of reaffirming his determination to quit smoking.

Then he saw it was anguish indeed, so extreme that Shaaban, recoiling and spinning about, stumbled back and fell rolling down the steps. The King was shocked. He was about to go after him when there was a flash of flame from his aide's hand. Instinctively Jalal flung himself down.

The explosion was the loudest the King had ever heard: a terrific roar that tore the air apart, rolling up the steps and shattering the thick glass doors at the top and washing back down again, knocking people flat all along the way. In a closed room it would have killed everyone at the table. Fortunately Shaaban was alone. The explosion tossed him up and flung him down the steps as if he were a rag doll, leaving parts of him scattered here and there.

The King lay flat a moment until he was sure he was safe. Then he rose, feeling himself to see if he was all right. His ears were ringing and he was stunned.

Just then he noticed the commotion on the sidewalk at the bottom of the steps, and he recognized David Morgan struggling in the arms of a group of soldiers. He began to realize what had happened, and as he hurried down to rescue his friend, he breathed a prayer of thanks.

"*Al hamdu, Lilah, al aly al azim* . . . Thanks to you, my Allah, the greatest and the savior."

The air was still shuddering. The bomb blast seemed to have set the whole city aquiver. Raising his eyes the King saw a flock of pigeons rising and circling above the sunken plaza across the street.

19

Page was troubled and Morgan knew it. But it wasn't until they got back to his room at the Tamanaco that he learned why.

He had phoned in a story of the assassination attempt to the *Globe* earlier and had promised to get back to them later that day with a wrap-up piece. He had decided to wait until then before mentioning Cuyakiare. It gave him great satisfaction to know that he could sit on the story as long as he wished and nobody would know the difference. It made him, he realized, unbearably gloating toward his rivals.

Once that day he had emerged from the Interior Minister's office where he, Joaquín, the King and Page were closeted, and had found Frank Taylor of the London *Telegraph* sweating it out in the hall with the other reporters.

"What are you up to now, Taffy?" Taylor had said.

"I imagine you'd like to know," Morgan said.

"Don't be silly, I enjoy standing out here in the dark."

"If you think it's dark now, wait until next week. It'll be a regular eclipse."

Morgan had always tried to curb any feelings of overweening ambition he might have. Newsmen weren't movie stars after all. They were hated and used by politicians, which often produced a desire for revenge. A good newsman's instinct for the jugular could invariably be traced back to the first time he had been booted out of a bigwig's office as a cub reporter for having asked an impertinent question.

But now Morgan couldn't help seeing his horizons widening. "We've got a lot to do," he said to Page as they drove to the Tamanaco.

She was silent. It had been a rough two days for her, he reflected. "You've got the film?"

"Yes," she said.

"We wouldn't want to lose that. As soon as we clean up, I'll call Kim Fuad at the U.P. and ask if we can use their darkroom. I imagine he'll wonder what we're being so secretive about. We'll have to tell him we're developing pornographic pictures."

Page smiled wearily without enthusiasm. Morgan had the feeling he was talking to himself.

"I'm sure they'll turn out. The camera doesn't seem to have been damaged any."

They arrived at the Tamanaco. Up in his room he took her in his arms, patting her rear end, fetchingly outlined by the dungarees she had worn into the jungle.

"Tired?"

She drew a deep breath and let it out, nodding. Then, impulsively she kissed him. There was something final and regretful about the kiss, as if it were the last he could expect from her for a long time. Just as abruptly she turned away.

Morgan felt the stubble of his beard. "I need a shave . . . " But he knew it wasn't that.

He looked at his watch. Two-thirty. That meant it was six-thirty in London. He had half an hour to make the first edition.

"Well, I've got to phone in that wrap-up piece."

He had already blocked the piece out in his head. It was a simple matter of tying up loose ends.

How was the King taking it? As well as could be expected. Jalal was tough. He would weather it.

Who would his new successor be? A good question. There was always the chance, as Karim had feared, that he might remarry, and rumor had it he was still remarkably potent for a man his age. But he also had a niece from his late wife's side of the family. An intelligent and attractive girl, Morgan had heard. She was planning to go to college in the United States next fall. The announcement had caused criticism from those who believed it was improper for a female of the Royal House to want an education. But she was popular with the people. Morgan wouldn't be surprised if El Hajjaz one day had a queen.

He proceeded to tie up loose ends even though he knew it required a bit of conjuring. Jules Smith had last been reported getting off a plane in Libya. Sooner or later he was bound to show up in one country or another.

The authorities were attempting to track down all those who had been involved in the conspiracy. The ambulance had been found and they were trying to trace it. Morgan had been purposely misleading about Emiliano's death. He had fallen from the mountain with Karim, he said, and his body had been lost while being brought downriver. He didn't want anyone nosing around the Autana. The Interior Minister, Octavio Lepage, had accepted the story without question. He was grateful the King was alive.

One loose end would remain forever dangling if Morgan had anything to say about it. Lepage had arranged to fly Joaquín back to the jungle immediately to avoid any publicity.

Morgan the sleight-of-hand artist prepared to make his phone call. He was still talking more or less to himself.

"Wait till Don Gordon hears what I've got for him. Of course, he won't believe it. He'll think I'm having him on. He'll need plenty of time to get ready. But it's going to take me a few days anyway to do the stories. I'll need some help from you on the scientific aspects. Then we'll fly up to New York and you can call a press conference. I imagine you'll want to have it at the museum. I wonder what your brother will say."

He laughed. This was going to be fun.

"It won't be long before your face is on the cover of *Time* and *Newsweek,*" he told her. "How will it feel to be famous?"

She didn't answer. She was emptying the pockets of her bush jacket, pensively removing the yellow packs of film, which she had numbered, and placing them on the bureau with her camera. One by one they constituted an unfolding sequence.

Roll one: The first shot would be the one she had taken from the Mooney when they were flying over the jungle, a scintillant brown river winding through it, unavoidably blurred by the plastic windowpane. She remembered the angry silence between them. Morgan had shook his finger at her. "I was shot at!" She had sat there feeling injured, her camera in her lap. But by the end of the roll, after pictures of the Makiritare and the village, there would be one of Morgan, standing dripping in his undershorts, and he would be smiling.

Roll two: The fight with the alligator. Shots of going upriver and several, taken by Joaquín from the bottom of the practice cliff, of her getting a climbing lesson from Morgan. The Autana in the distance, solitary and grand. Joaquín raising his blowpipe to his lips in a pose she had asked for while they were having breakfast the next morning. And finally Morgan and her together with their arms around each other at the base of the mountain before they began to climb.

Roll three: Shots on the wall, showing them individually, as they handed the camera back and forth, hanging from ropes, placing pitons, mugging defiantly as the jungle got farther away. One stuck out in her memory, the result of a suggestion she had made before they resumed climbing the morning after making love in the bat tent. "Don't you think we should take a picture to commemorate the spot," she said. She had blown a kiss and the shutter had clicked. Then the glee at thinking they were the first to set foot atop the Autana. She had clowned, doing a jig on the grass between the clumps of yellow pitcher plants with the whole world spread out below.

Roll four: This was the crucial one. The shots of the cave would be stunning if the colors turned out. The entrance as seen from within, a magnificent frame that dwarfed Morgan standing in it, looking out. Or Morgan posed on a heap of geological rubble with the orange dome rising in concentric circles behind and above him. Then there would be a break in the sequence. Nothing would prepare you for what came next. She saw the face as she had framed it in the viewfinder. It would be as famous as Morgan had said hers would soon be. And then what?

She placed the last pack of film next to the others, identical. If you didn't know, you would never guess the blown kiss was in roll three.

"What's wrong?" Morgan asked her.

She removed her bush jacket and hung it on the back of the bureau chair. "I don't know, I guess it's just that I'm not all that happy about what we're going to do."

He misunderstood her. "I don't blame you. Having all those microphones thrust at you wherever you go. But you'll get used to it."

"It's not me I'm worried about."

"Who are you worried about? Me? Why would you be worried about——"

"Of course not. It's Cuyakiare."

He looked at her. "I don't get it."

"Don't you see what's going to happen to him?"

Morgan didn't like the way the conversation was going. "I can't say that I've given it much thought. I'm sure——"

"Don't you see that the minute the world learns about him it'll be the end of him?"

He got it now and he didn't like it. "What are you proposing?"

"I'm proposing that we leave him alone."

"You mean not tell anybody about him?"

"Well," she said, "certainly not the whole world."

"I see." He attempted a joke. "You're suggesting we keep him from the Communists. Like a secret weapon." Then, nonchalantly, as if the matter were dropped, "I think I'll have a drink. Want anything?"

She shook her head, turning away. He went to the phone on the bed table and picked up the receiver. Page sat down on the end of one of the two beds. Her back accused him. Morgan got room service, ordered his drink and hung up.

"You don't want to break the story," he said flatly to the back.

"That's right."

"You want to keep it a secret."

"To all except a few."

"What few?"

"My brother and a few others."

"Fine. What's wrong with my friends and relatives?"

"Mine will appreciate him."

"What the hell do you mean by that?"

They were facing each other now and Page looked up at him apologetically. "Oh, David, you know what I mean."

"I'm not sure I do."

"Cuyakiare should be studied by people who are concerned for his welfare, not just interested in making a circus of his life."

"Who's making a circus of his life? This isn't some trivial item of gossip. This is the biggest story of my career."

"Yes, and the minute you publish it he'll be as good as dead."

He couldn't deny what she said and Page knew it.

"You know as well as I do," she said. "They'll never leave him alone. They'll be selling Cuyakiare T-shirts and Cuyakiare wind-up toys at the bottom of the Autana."

"He would have eaten us," Morgan grumbled, "if he hadn't had his fill."

"Well, that would have been his privilege. We were invading his world."

"His world is dead. This is the twentieth century."

"You wouldn't be so casual if it were the Makiritare. Didn't you say in your book that one Makiritare was worth half the civilized people you knew?"

"That damn book." Morgan paced. Where the hell was his drink? He looked at his watch again. He was going to miss the first edition.

"Have you stopped to think what will happen to the Indians when people start flocking down there?" Page said.

His head jerked around. He considered her soberly.

"I hate to keep reminding you of your book," she added, "since you've been at such pains to disown it ever since I met you. But didn't you also say that the Makiritare way of life is as fragile as it is strong? That one breath of civilization would corrode it?"

"Then it can't be helped. Nothing goes on forever."

"You're not such a fatalist as you pretend."

"I don't care." He flung up his arms and resumed pacing. "I can't do it. It's against everything I believe." He whirled, pointing at her with indignation. "Do you realize what you're suggesting?"

"What?"

From the headlines he produced a fashionably unassailable argument. "A cover-up. You want to hide the truth."

"It's not the truth. It's just the news."

Morgan reacted as if wounded. "Just the news!"

She glared at him. "Didn't you once tell me that all newsmen were vultures who feed off the carrion of events?"

He glared back. She was being unfair, using against him some silly self-deprecating remark he had made in an idle moment and only half meant.

Woman reads book. Believes nonsense about dinosaur. Forces him to go into jungle with her. Climb the Autana. Captured by terrorists. Face firing squad. Saved by dinosaur. Not nonsense after all. He had to tell the world. Couldn't keep Cuyakiare locked up inside his head. Nothing to eat in there except brains. Could see brains being gobbled up by Cuyakiare until he, Morgan, was completely empty-headed, confirming a state his friends and acquaintances had long speculated about. People would gaze into his blank, staring eyes and there Cuyakiare would be, peering out at them. Then they would know. Couldn't hide it from the world. Can't. Won't. Impossible.

His eyes fell on the four packs of film on the bureau. He had a mind to grab roll four and walk out. But hell, he didn't need her pictures. He could go back to the Autana and take his own. Of course, she was right, Cuyakiare would be done for . . .

He thought of roll three and his gaze lingered as if he had forgotten which was the crucial pack. Was it three or four? He hesitated. Three or four? The choice was postponed by a knock on the door.

He went to it muttering. "Damn dinosaur . . ."

At the door a waiter stood holding a tray in one hand with a scotch on the rocks on it. Morgan let him in, following him into the room. The waiter placed the tray on the bureau and produced a check. Morgan searched for a pen, still muttering.

". . . studied by people who are concerned for his welfare . . ."

He began to swear. He couldn't find his pen. He had brought one into the jungle with him. Where the hell . . . then he remembered Karim had taken it from him on the Autana.

The waiter came to his rescue, handing him a pencil. Morgan

signed the check and began to swear again as he fumbled in his pockets for a tip. He found a bill and stuffed it in the waiter's hand, followed him to the door and closed it.

When he turned back to Page, with a scowl he couldn't restrain, he had made his choice. He didn't like it, but it was the only one he could live with. It was her dinosaur after all. She had raced beneath its colossal knees to photograph it.

She was still sitting on the end of the bed, unbuttoning her shirt, getting ready to take a shower. No overweening ambition in her, that's for sure. A solid piece of work. But hell, Morgan thought, you've always known that, even before she climbed the Autana.

Still, it was a hard choice for him to make and there was one thing, as he came back into the room, that he intended to make clear.

"Listen," he said levelly, "newsmen might be vultures and events might be carrion. But events are what the world is made of. You'll never escape that."

Page looked up at him, chagrined. She sensed from his tone that he had given in, and she was sad. She knew what she was asking him to give up.

"You know," he said with the fatalistic cheerfulness of a professional soldier losing a battle, "I've never sat on a story in my life."

"Yes you have," she said.

"What story?"

"Joaquín. You've never told who his mother is."

Morgan laughed. That made losing all the easier. "Joaquín is my friend," he said.

"So," she said, "Cuyakiare is my friend. I'll trade you a friend for a friend."

She rose and went into the bathroom to shower, to wash off the dust of the Autana. A moment later Morgan went after her to tell her he had met his match.

PS
3565
.W56
E9
1978

$15.95

PS
3565
.W56
E9

1978